D0966275

The Best of
Scary Stories for Stormy Nights

The Best of

SCARY STORIES

for Stormy Nights

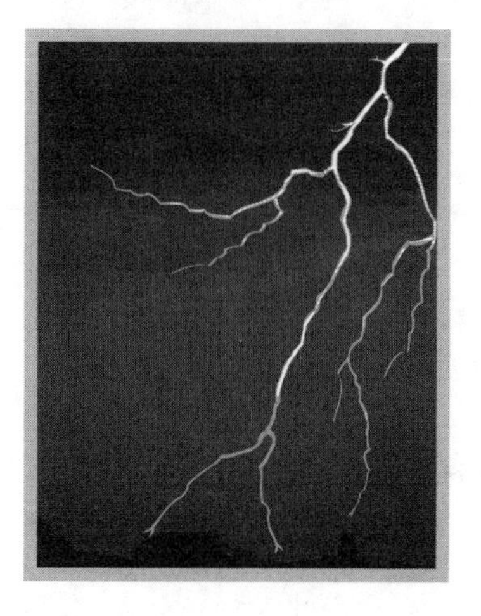

LOWELL HOUSE JUVENILE

LOS ANGELES

NTC/Contemporary Publishing Group

Published by Lowell House
A division of NTC/Contemporary Publishing Group, Inc.
4255 West Touhy Avenue
Lincolnwood (Chicago), Illinois 60712-1975 U.S.A.

Lowell House books can be purchased at special discounts when ordered in balk for premiums and special sales. Contact Department CS at the following address:

NTC/Contemporary Publishing Group
4255 West Touhy Avenue
Lincolnwood, IL 60712-1975
1-800-323-4900

ISBN: 0-7373-0431-6
Library of Congress Control Number: 00-133248
Roxbury Park is a division of NTC/Contemporary Publishing Group, Inc.

Managing Director and Publisher: Jack Artenstein
Editor in Chief, Roxbury Park Books: Michael Artenstein
Director of Publishing Services: Rena Copperman
Senior Editor: Maria Magallanes
Editorial Assistant: Nicole Monastirsky
Interior Design: Robert S. Tinnon Design
Cover Art: Greg Thorkelson

Printed and bound in the United States of America
00 01 02 DHD 10 9 8 7 6 5 4 3 2 1

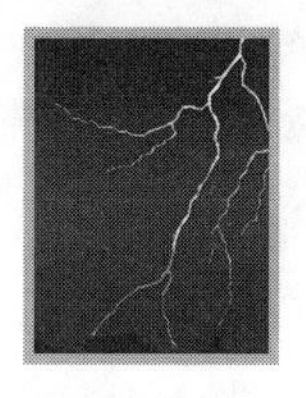

CONTENTS

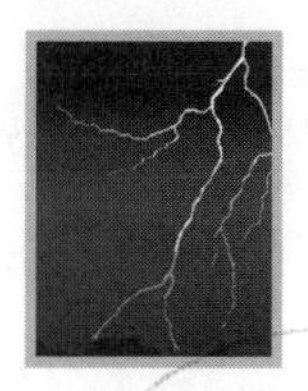

SHOPLIFTERS WILL BE KILLED AND EATEN

Mark Kehl

All day Douglas looked forward to one thing: making his weekly trip to Memories of Tomorrow after school. Today was Tuesday, and every Tuesday Memories, the town's best comic book and trading card store, received its shipment of new comics and other merchandise.

Douglas's friends and classmates would be lined up for the new comics, but comics didn't interest Douglas. He loved dinosaurs. He watched movies about them, read books about them, and built models of them. The walls of his room were covered with dinosaur posters. His shelves were packed with dinosaur action figures. He even had dinosaur sheets on his bed. His greatest dream was that someday he would be a paleontologist, studying dinosaurs—or at least what was left of them—firsthand.

Half the items in his room had come from Memories of Tomorrow, but it had been a while since the store had gotten anything new for him to buy. In his opinion, Stephen, the owner and manager, gave too much of his attention to comics and science fiction books and not enough to dinosaurs.

Stephen was famous for being able to get almost anything his customers wanted, no matter how old or how hard to find. He had gotten a rare early *Superman* comic for Jimmy Feldman's dad, and in excellent condition. Stephen himself had a signed first edition of H. G. Wells's classic science fiction novel *The Time Machine* on display in the store, though it wasn't for sale. If he could get things like that, how hard could it be to get a few new dinosaur-related items every week? Douglas was a good customer and deserved good treatment.

After school, he rode his bike to the town square, where numerous colorful shops surrounded the historic courthouse. Then he turned onto a side street and chained his bicycle to a parking meter in front of Santino's Italian Restaurant. Next to the restaurant entrance, a set of concrete steps led down. A hand-painted sign with an arrow pointing downward read: MEMORIES OF TOMORROW.

Douglas descended the steps, feeling a familiar surge of anticipation. This could be the week! He pushed his way into the store and lingered around the front by the T-shirt rack while his eyes adjusted to the dimness. Since it was below street level, the store had no windows, and it was lit by only a few fluorescent lights. Countless posters covered the walls, where they were visible, and shelves displaying comics, paperbacks, models, and all sorts of other merchandise packed most of the available floor space. A row of glass cases formed a counter on one side, behind which Stephen worked. He and his assistant, Carl, were dealing with the line of people there to buy newly acquired comics, but he waved when he saw Douglas.

"Hey, buddy," he called. "I have a little something you might be interested in."

Douglas made his way to the counter as Stephen rooted around behind it. Stephen was a tall, thin man with a long, dark ponytail and a goatee. He usually wore T-shirts with comic book characters on them, like the Spawn shirt he was wearing today.

"We finally got the *Dino-Fever* cards," Stephen said as he searched. "Those are already out on the floor. But there was—aha!"

He stood from behind the counter and unrolled a poster for Douglas's inspection.

"Wow, T. Rex!" Douglas cheered. But as he studied the king of the dinosaurs, something struck him as wrong. "It's blue," he said.

Stephen looked at the poster and shrugged. "Yeah, but look at the quality of the artwork. Reynolds Sinclair painted this image. It's a hundred times better than those other posters you've bought."

"Yeah," Douglas said, "but it's blue."

"Sure it's blue," Stephen said. "Look, you're up on your dinosaur reading. You know that scientists don't really know what color dinosaurs were. All they've got are bones."

"Yeah, but T. Rex was not blue," Douglas protested. "It just doesn't look right."

"You've seen Jurassic Park too many times, buddy," Stephen told him, getting a laugh from the dozen people standing in line for comics.

"I have not," Douglas said, feeling his face turn red.

Stephen let the poster roll closed and held up one hand in a gesture of peace. "Okay, okay. If you don't want the poster, that's fine. But I know you plan on being a paleontologist. I've had some scientific training myself, and I'll tell you, if you're going to be a scientist, you've got to keep an open mind. And I'll tell you something else—Tyrannosaurus Rex *really was* blue."

"Yeah, right, Stephen," Douglas said, turning away. "Like you know everything."

"No, not everything," Stephen said with a theatrical flourish of his hands, "but I do know an excellent poster when I see one, my close-minded little friend."

The people in line laughed louder this time. Douglas snorted and walked away. His skin burned with anger and embarrassment.

Stephen doesn't know what he's talking about, Douglas told himself. *He just likes to show off. See if I ever buy anything else here again*.

But as he headed for the door, he passed a rack containing boxes of all sorts of trading cards, including the new *Dino-Fever* cards. He bit his lip as he picked up one of the foil-wrapped packets. He had read about the cards and seen ads in magazines, but he hadn't been able to find them anywhere. The sample cards pictured in the ads looked really cool, and Douglas yearned to see what the rest of the cards looked like. But he didn't want to give Stephen the satisfaction of getting his money or another chance to make fun of him.

Douglas glanced at the counter, but Stephen wasn't paying any attention to him. He was too busy filling comic book orders and laughing with other customers—probably about Douglas.

Douglas slipped the cards into his jacket pocket.

Nothing happened. No bells or alarms, no shouts of "Stop, thief!" The light was so dim in the store that Stephen probably couldn't even make out his face, much less what he was doing.

Douglas grabbed a handful of packets and stuck them in his pocket. Then he put another handful in his other pocket. He smiled at Stephen, who still didn't notice him, and at the stupid sign Stephen had hanging behind the counter that said "Shoplifters will be killed and eaten."

Then he turned and left the store. He walked back up the stairs to his bicycle. As he pedaled home, he thought not only about his many new *Dino-Fever* cards, but also about how he had gotten even with that smug jerk Stephen.

For the next couple of days, Douglas was nervous about having stolen the cards. Whenever he heard a car door slam outside his house, he thought it was the police coming to take him away. By the next Tuesday, he was getting over his guilt but still didn't go back to Memories of Tomorrow. He told himself it was because he thought Stephen was a jerk, but there was also a guilty fear in him that, as soon as he walked in, Stephen would accuse him of stealing the cards.

But by the Tuesday after that, Douglas thought he was safe. There was no way that Stephen had seen what he had done, and he had so much stuff in his store he probably had no idea anything was even missing. Besides, Douglas had spent two whole weeks with no new dinosaur stuff, and he was itching to go see if he could find something interesting at Memories. And though he had stolen quite a few cards, he still needed a few to complete his set. This time he would actually pay for them—unless Stephen was a jerk again.

Douglas left his bike chained to the parking meter and went into the store. It didn't seem to have changed at all in two weeks. The usual Tuesday afternoon crowd was there waiting for their new comics, and Stephen and Carl were busy behind the counter. Douglas started to look around, hoping that Stephen wouldn't notice him.

"Hey, buddy," Stephen called. "Good to see you. We missed you last week."

Douglas walked toward the counter. "Yeah, I wasn't feeling too good."

"It figures—the one week we get something I know you're going to be interested in."

Douglas felt the stirrings of disappointment. He knew he should have come in last week. Stephen didn't suspect a thing about his shoplifting the cards. Now, because of his guilty conscience, he had missed something good.

"What was it?" Douglas asked, now not sure if he even wanted to know.

Stephen gave him a sparkling smile. "Cheer up! I saved it for you. Come on, it's in back."

Stephen told Carl he'd be back in a minute and then came around the counter to lead Douglas through the store to the stout door in the rear. Stephen flipped through a ring of keys. Douglas glanced back at the others in the store, suddenly nervous. He had heard Carl talking one day when Stephen wasn't in the store. Someone asked about this door, and Carl said that nobody was allowed through it; even he didn't know what was behind it. So why would Stephen show Douglas what was on the other side? Did it have something to do with his shoplifting? Was Stephen going to hold him back there until he confessed? Douglas wanted to bolt out of the store, but that would really look suspicious. Before he could decide what to do, Stephen had the door open and was ushering him through.

On the other side was a workroom. Tools of all sorts, from heavy hammers to complex electronic measuring devices, lined the walls and cluttered workbenches. Boxes filled with odd bits of hardware and electronics were tucked wherever there was room. But Douglas didn't have much time to look around. Stephen led him across the room to another door and into the room beyond. This second room was small, no more than 10 feet square, with bare walls painted silver. The only furniture in the room was a small desk by the door with a computer on it. Stephen sat down at the computer and started to type.

"Douglas," he said as he typed, "I believe I owe you an apology for the last time you were here. I can be a little thick-headed sometimes, but after you didn't come last week I realized that you were probably angry with me and that you had every right to be."

An apology was the last thing Douglas had expected, and in his relief he rushed to accept it. "That's okay, really."

"No," Stephen said, "no, it's not. But I'm going to make it up to you." He turned and smiled at Douglas. "Right now." He tapped one final key, and it felt as if the whole building had jumped. Douglas staggered, looking around wildly as if the roof might cave in, but everything was still.

"What was that?" Douglas asked.

"That," Stephen answered as he stood, "is a secret. One I'm going to share with you. Come on."

He opened the door and led Douglas back out into the workroom—only it wasn't a workroom anymore. The bare basement room was empty except for a table and a couple of wooden boxes. Stephen picked up two long overcoats from the table and tossed one to Douglas.

"Put that on," he said. "It's going to be a good deal colder outside than you remember. It will help hide your clothes too."

Douglas was confused but did as he was told, slipping into the heavy woolen coat and buttoning the old-fashioned buttons. "Why do I need to hide my clothes?" he asked.

"So they don't draw unwanted attention," Stephen answered. "Come along."

He led Douglas through the other door back into the store—only the store was also gone. The basement here was empty except for a large pile of coal and a monstrous iron furnace that glowed with heat.

"My secret is this," Stephen said as he led Douglas across the room. "You know how I'm able to find so many rare old treasures for so many of my customers?"

They started up the steps to street level.

"Yes," Douglas said.

"I do it by going back in time, to when those items were new and easy to come by. That room behind the store is a time machine."

They reached the top of the steps. Douglas's bike was gone, the parking meters were gone, the Italian restaurant was gone. It was snowing, though it had been 70 degrees when Douglas had arrived at the store. The cars that lined the street looked enormous and overinflated, like cars out of an old movie.

"Welcome," Stephen said, "to the 1940s."

Stephen led the way up the street toward the courthouse. Douglas marveled at how the square was so different and yet still so familiar. The old movie theater that had burned down years ago was all lit up and was advertising a new John Wayne film. The traffic lights at the main intersection were gone, replaced by a policeman directing traffic in an old-fashioned uniform. On one corner was a wooden newsstand Douglas had never seen before, and that was Stephen's destination.

"Good day, Mr. Fink," Stephen said to the man behind the counter.

"And to you too, sir," answered the man, digging beneath the counter. "I've got your order right here. Though what a grown man like yourself sees in these funny books is beyond me."

He handed over a small bundle bound with string. On top Douglas saw a new copy of a *Batman* comic book.

"They're not for me," Stephen said, handing the man some money. "They're for a . . . friend."

"Sure, they are," the man answered. "You keep yourself warm tonight, sir. It's supposed to be a cold one. A good night to stay in and listen to the radio by the fire."

Stephen thanked the man and then led Douglas back toward the store—or to where the store would be in 50 years.

"This is amazing," Douglas said as they walked. "How long have you been doing this?"

"A few years," Stephen answered as they walked. "I was studying physics in college and came up with my theory of time travel. After I got it working, I realized I could do whatever I wanted, and what I really wanted was to open up a comic book shop. Since then, I've traveled in time to find items for my customers and just for my own enlightenment. It's fascinating, the things you can learn."

They reached their building and returned to the basement. Following Stephen's example, Douglas took off his heavy overcoat and left it on the table. Then both went back into the time-travel room. Stephen sat down at the computer and began to type. When he finished, the room again seemed to jump. He directed Douglas to the door. Douglas opened it and stepped outside.

He had expected to find himself back in the workroom, but instead he found himself outside in a steamy jungle. He sank to his ankles in the marshy ground and found himself surrounded by the fronds of gigantic ferns. The buzz of insects filled the air. He glanced back, where the doorway into the time-travel room appeared to float in midair. Stephen stood in the doorway, holding a small gun pointed at Douglas!

"Don't worry," Stephen said, waving the gun. "I'm a man of my word, and I promise not to hurt you. I just want to make sure I have your complete attention. You probably haven't had enough time to consider all the ramifications of time travel, so allow me to point out another use. When I discovered that someone had stolen a whole pile of *Dino-Fever* cards from my store, I went back in time and hid a video camera to catch the thief in the act."

The ground shook, but not from travel through time. Douglas looked around but could see nothing through the thick vegetation.

"Perhaps you've noticed the sign in my shop," Stephen continued conversationally. "The one that says 'SHOPLIFTERS WILL BE KILLED AND EATEN'?" He glanced around as the trembling of the ground grew stronger, and he smiled. "As I said, I'm a man of my word."

He stepped back and started to shut the door. Douglas screamed for him to stop, but a split second later the door closed and vanished completely. Douglas waved his hands through the air where it had been but felt nothing.

Then the ground stopped shaking. He turned and looked up. A huge, menacing form loomed over him, with mighty jaws filled with countless razorlike teeth. As the teeth descended toward him, Douglas coldly realized that Stephen had been right: Tyrannosaurus Rex really was blue.

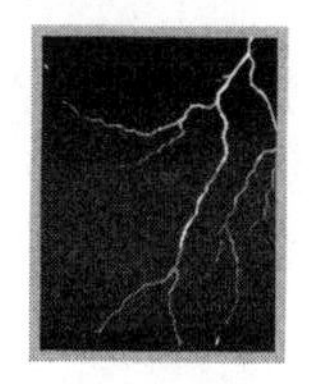

MILLER'S POINT

Jonathon Schmidt

Becka sat up in bed. She swung her legs over the side and stretched. It was the first day of summer vacation, and Becka couldn't wait to shower and eat and head down to the beach to meet her friends. This would be the best summer ever. First off, next term she would be a 10th grader. No more baby stuff for her.

Second, it was pretty much common knowledge that Matt Hastings had a crush on her. And Matt was just about the best-looking boy in San Diego.

But best of all, she was part of The Group. Only the prettiest and most popular girls at James Madison were asked to join The Group. The crème de la crème. The elite.

But when she looked over at the guest bed across the room she frowned, as if suddenly remembering something horrible.

Marianne.

Her cousin had arrived last night. She was from Iowa. Becka had never met anyone from Iowa before. Iowa sounded as far away and as bleak as Mars.

A few weeks earlier her mother had asked Becka if it would be all right for Becka's cousin to come and stay the summer. It wasn't fair, Becka whined "You won't have to baby-sit," her mother said. "Marianne is the same age as you. You and she will have a lot in common."

Becka let her chin drop. She rolled her gorgeous blue eyes to the sky and groaned: "Oh really, mother. I mean, have you gone, like, completely eight-track? The little tumor is from Idaho."

"Iowa."

"What . . . *ever*."

"I want you to be nice to her. Show her around. You two will have loads of fun together. Introduce her to your friends."

"Are you like totally *insane*?" Becka shrieked. "I'd rather die first." This was just the kind of hideous infraction that could get a member expelled from The Group.

"Oh, Becka, quit being so dramatic. Now go upstairs and clean your room. And clear out your closet to make space for Marianne."

"*She's staying in my room?*"

"Yes, dear." The guest room was being refurnished, and Mrs. Hoover didn't want Marianne inconvenienced by having to share space with sawhorses and paint buckets and drop cloths. "Remember, it's only for the summer."

Suddenly Becka's sunny pastel-colored dream-come-true summer darkened into a stormy rain-drenched nightmare named . . .

Marianne.

She arrived last night from the airport. It was dinnertime, but Marianne said she was too tired to eat, and asked if it would be okay to go straight to bed.

Becka's mother smiled and got up to ready the bed in Becka's room.

Marianne looked alarmed. "No," she said anxiously, "I'll do it."

Becka watched her carry the sheets and blanket upstairs. But on the landing Marianne stopped momentarily, her foot above the stair tread. She turned and looked back at Becka and grinned. It gave Becka a chill.

That night Becka phoned all her friends but only got their answering machines. *Strange*, she thought, *were they all out together*? She felt panicky. What if they had seen her with Marianne? What if they no longer wanted her in The Group?

The rain began early the next morning and continued throughout the day. Becka took Marianne to the mall to look for new shoes. She told her mother she wanted to go to the Mission Hills Mall.

"But that's so far away."

Becka shrugged. The truth was she didn't want to go anywhere her friends might see her with Marianne.

The mall was pretty crowded. They poked around a bunch of shops and then had lunch. Becka had a yogurt with granola. Marianne had some rice and chicken. As they got up to leave, Becka noticed that Marianne had hardly eaten any of her lunch. She had swept it up quickly and dropped the carton into the trash.

"Not hungry?"

Marianne shook her head and smiled wanly.

What a weirdo, thought Becka.

Becka had strange dreams throughout the night. When she woke up the next morning she felt vaguely uneasy. It was as if someone had been watching her through her bedroom window.

Marianne was already awake. The guest bed was made. Becka looked out the window. It had stopped raining; the sun was shining and the sky was a brilliant deep blue.

She could hear the hissing of the shower in the bathroom down the hall.

She took a few steps across the carpet and yelped, pulling herself up on her toes. The carpet was sopping wet! A damp trail of footprints led from the guest bed out the door. Footprints crusted with sand.

Becka thought, *Marianne?*

She tiptoed down the hall to the bathroom. The door was closed, and she tapped lightly. "Marianne? Marianne, are you in there?" She was just about to knock again when the door opened a few inches from the inside. The air was foggy with steam. The shower was hissing at full blast.

"Marianne?" said Becka, fanning away the steam with her hands.

A voice behind her whispered, "Here I am."

Becka whirled and screamed. "Ah! Marianne, you scared me to death. What's your problem, sneaking up behind me like that? And why is the water still running? Don't you know there is, like, a water shortage?"

Marianne stared at her, unblinking. Then she smiled. It was a smile that pulled sideways across her teeth like a slash and didn't curl up at the ends. Her jet black hair was parted in the middle and hung in long damp strands over her face. She stared at Becka through black eyes as flat and hard as polished marble.

"Did you go to the beach this morning?" asked Becka.

"No."

Becka cocked one hip and put a finger to her lips. She affected a sarcastic tone. Sarcasm was the weapon of choice among members of The Group. "Really? Gee, I wonder how come there are soggy sandy footprints on the carpet? Hmmmm."

Marianne shrugged.

Becka flung open the door of the shower. Swatting at a cloud of steam, she turned to Marianne accusingly.

"Explain this."

The tiles were covered with swirling eddies of sand, and tangled threads of seaweed clogged the drain.

Marianne's cold grin deepened, and Becka suddenly

felt herself on the defensive. An unpleasant aroma like hot sour breath caressed her face and made her stomach roll unsteadily.

Marianne finally broke off her gaze, turned sideways, and slipped passed Becka.

Becka showered and put on her favorite new bathing suit and slipped on a pair of baggy shorts and a cropped T-shirt. The she went downstairs for breakfast.

Marianne was reading a book and sipping a cup of tea. She was tall, and thin as a pole. Her shaggy black hair had been pulled through a bright red-and-white scrunchie. Her long skinny arms and legs reminded Becka of an insect's. Her skin was pale blue, like milk. Under each eye were dark crescents.

"What are you reading?" asked Becka.

"*Crime and Punishment*. Dostoevsky."

"Sounds boring," Becka shrugged. She watched Marianne slowly turn a page in her book. She reminded Becka of a corpse. *I can even see her veins*.

Her mother came out of the kitchen with bowls of fruit and cereal.

"Nothing for me," said Marianne. "I don't like to eat."

Becka dropped her spoon. "What do you mean you don't like to eat? Everybody eats. What are you, some kind of vampire or something?"

Her mother glared at her. "What your cousin means is, she's not hungry." Then she turned to Marianne. "But you really should eat something, Marianne. You've hardly eaten since you've been here. It isn't my cooking, is it? Because if there is something special you want, that's no problem."

Marianne said, "Maybe a piece of toast." She smiled sweetly.

Becka tried calling her friends. But once again all she could do was leave messages on their machines. She was coming out of the family room when she bumped into Marianne, who was wearing a beautiful necklace with a tear drop pearl pendant.

"Where did you get that?"

Marianne fingered the pearl absently, then said, "I got it at the mall, when you were busy making phone calls. Do you like it?"

Becka narrowed her eyes. "I guess. It looks like a pearl necklace that belongs to my best friend, Monica."

"What are you suggesting?"

Becka shook her head, "Nothing."

Later Becka was talking with her mother in the laundry room. They were downstairs in the basement. The air was warm and smelled of soap.

"Help me fold these," her mother said, bundling some towels from the dryer. "Your cousin is from Iowa. I guess they do things differently there."

"I'll say."

Her mother frowned at Becka. "Be nice to her. Marianne doesn't make friends easily. She's very shy." Her mother looked away and then let out her breath. "Apparently Marianne has a few . . . problems."

Becka snorted. "No kidding. The girl is a total nut job."

"She's a perfectly sweet girl."

Becka shot her a you-must-be-kidding glance. "What about the not eating thing?"

"She's self-conscious about her figure."

"What figure? She doesn't have a figure. She doesn't sleep either."

"Not everyone needs 16 hours of sleep, Becka." Her mother looked at her reprovingly, then turned away.

"She smells. I mean she really smells. She stinks like dead fish and old seaweed."

"That's enough, young lady."

"But she does! It's, like, totally gross."

"I said *enough*. For the last week I've endured your constant whining and complaining, and I'm sick of it. Okay? Beginning right now you'll start treating Marianne as a guest in this house. And I mean you will be on your absolute best behavior. Or else. Do you understand me?"

The next day Marianne found Becka sitting on the front porch.

"You want to go to the beach?" asked Marianne. She had a different scrunchie on this morning. Becka thought it looked familiar. Then she realized it was exactly the same one that she had given Alicia for her birthday.

"Okay."

It was a short walk to the beach. They reached the crest of a fenced bluff, then walked down a steep path that wound through a canyon.

Along the way, Marianne turned to Becka.

"I'm sorry about all this. I know my coming here has ruined your summer. And I completely understand how bad it must be for you. I've ruined everything for you. Believe me, I know what it's like not to be able to hang out with friends. I don't blame you for hating me."

Becka was stunned. "It's not like I *hate* you, exactly."

Marianne nodded, "It's okay. I was just hoping that we might be friends."

Before Becka had a chance to take it back, she said, "Okay."

The sky was overcast, and the glare of the sun turned the sea into a polished sheet of metal. The beach was deserted except for a few mothers and their kids camped under umbrellas that sprouted in the sand like rainbow-colored mushrooms.

A boy with a surfboard walking along the edge of the beach called out to Becka. She smiled and waved. It was Matt. Another boy came loping out of the surf behind Matt and joined him. Derrick Matthews.

"Wait here," Becka said coldly to Marianne. Then she walked over to talk with Matt and Derrick.

"Hey, Becka. Where've you been? And who's the ghoul?" asked Matt.

"My creepy cousin. That's why I haven't been around."

"Totally Morticia Adams," joked Derrick.

"No kidding. Hey, have you guys seen Alicia and Monica?"

Matt shook his head. "I thought they were with you."

"What about LizBeth?"

Matt shrugged.

Becka frowned. "Okay. Well, if you see them, tell them I'm baby-sitting The Ghoul."

Derrick asked, "Hey, you're not heading up toward Miller's Point, are you?"

Becka frowned. The truth was, Becka didn't want to risk her reputation by being seen with a loser like Marianne, even if it meant walking all the way to Miller's Point, where she was pretty sure they would be alone.

"I don't know. Maybe."

Matt narrowed his eyes. "But what about that girl who—you know . . . "

Becka sighed. "Look, that story is just a myth. That girl didn't kill herself off the point. It never happened. She was, like, a total emotional wreck. I heard she was sent away to some special school somewhere. Anyway, I gotta go." She shrugged her shoulders, smiled coyly at Matt, and walked back to Marianne.

They walked along the water's edge to where the beach made a wide curve. At the far end of the curve a tumble of huge rocks jutted out into the sea. Miller's Point.

"Tell me about the girl who killed herself," said Marianne.

Becka stopped dead in her tracks. Her eyes narrowed suspiciously. "Who told you about her? What do you know about it?"

Marianne shrugged, but Becka saw in her eyes a glint of triumph. "I just heard things. From kids in the neighborhood."

"You don't know any kids in the neighborhood."

Marianne sniffed haughtily. "It's just a story, right, Becka? It's not like you had anything to do with it."

"That's right. I didn't even really know the kid. She was in my class in fifth grade. I mean it's not like we were friends or anything."

They walked a long way. After a while the smooth sand turned pebbly and rough with rocks and boulders. Becka had never come this far up shore. At least, not since the girl's body had been discovered drowned in a pool by the rocks. Becka tried to forget, but that only made the memory more real. It was a harmless prank. Kids' stuff.

Becka couldn't even remember the girl's name.

All Becka could remember was that the girl didn't have any friends at all. Even The Untouchables shunned her. And they were so unpopular they would accept just about anyone.

But ever since the accident, the rocks at Miller's Point had become a kind of weird shrine to the girl's memory.

"This is far enough," said Becka. She threw down her pack, flipped out her blanket, and lay down. Marianne sat next to her in the sand. Becka couldn't believe that she didn't burn in the sun. Her skin was as white as cream.

Becka sat up, startled. "What did you say?"

Marianne squinted at her as she let a handful of sand run idly through her fingers. "Nothing, Becka. Go back to sleep."

Becka let out a long sighing breath.

The sun was coming out from behind the haze and it felt exhilarating on Becka's skin. She had the portable radio tuned to her favorite station. All she needed was her real friends and it would be a perfect day. She tried to concentrate on forgetting about Marianne. After a while she squinted her eyes and peeked sideways at Marianne. Marianne had her knees pulled up, and her chin rested on her folded arms.

Becka shivered.

After a while the sun was making her drowsy, and before long the low drumming of the waves crowded out thoughts of Marianne, and Becka fell into a deep sleep.

She was awakened by a voice calling her name.

Becka sat up. The sand and sky were a ferocious white glare that stung her eyes. It took some time for them to adjust. *Where was Marianne?* She looked up and down the beach but saw no one.

Becka!

Becka corkscrewed one way. "Monica?" And then the other. "Alicia, where are you?" There was no one on the beach, but she heard her friends' voices calling her. *Where are they?* Becka walked down to the water's edge.

There she spun around and around. "Where are you?" An edge of panic crept into her voice. "Come on, you guys, this isn't funny! Tell me where you are!" She noticed a trail of footprints in the sand that lead along the beach to where the massive rock arch of Miller's Point jutted out into the sea.

"Monica?" she called out tentatively.

Becka, we're down here . . .

Reluctantly Becka slogged through the shallow sea water and climbed out onto the rocks. She stood up unsteadily and gazed down at the waves that looped and curled around the rocks. A swelling gust of wind rushed across the jagged rocks and clutched at her. She felt wobbly and had to steady herself with outstretched arms.

"Alicia? Monica?"

Becka was standing in front of a dark hollow formed by two rock slabs that tilted head to head. She nervously peered down into the hollow. It seemed to drop steeply, then stop and curve inward. Vaguely she could hear the muffled rumbling of waves sloshing back and forth inside.

We're in here.

Becka crouched and peered down. "Where? Where are you?"

A voice from behind made Becka whirl and scream.

"Here we are." It was Marianne. Her lips were stretched in a snarl. Becka was so frightened that she lost her footing and fell headlong down the mouth of the tunnel. Her head cracked hard on the rock.

When she regained consciousness she was staring up into the dome of an underwater cavern. Water misted on the ceiling and rained down in a steady rhythm. She slid up into a sitting position and dabbed the back of her head. A whispering voice rose like mist over the pool of water.

Becka looked up.

Marianne was backed up against the wall of rock, staring at her.

"What?" Becka heard herself ask groggily. The pungent stink of brackish water and rotting fish made her wince, and she thought she might vomit.

"I said, 'Nice of you to drop in.'"

Becka sobbed, "Is that supposed to be a joke?"

"Yes!" Marianne nodded thoughtfully. She stood up and walked over to Becka. Marianne gave her cousin a can-you-keep-a-secret grin, then whispered: "Maybe you would like to hear a little story?"

Becka shook her head, no. "That's too bad, because this is a really good story. And best of all, it's true. Once upon a time, there was a little girl who wanted to be popular. But none of the other girls liked her. They teased her and told her she was ugly and wouldn't let her play with them. And they wouldn't let other little girls play with her either. So the poor little girl had no friends at all."

Becka looked at Marianne and swallowed. It was like seeing an apparition in the fog slowly coming into focus.

"But that wasn't the worst of it. One day the popular girls thought it would be hilariously funny to play a trick on the poor little girl. They pretended they wanted to be friends with her. They even invited her to the beach. But the little girl had not grown up near the sea. She didn't know how to swim. 'That's okay,' they said. 'We'll teach you.' And the little girl believed them. Because that's how much she wanted to have friends."

Becka slowly shook her head. "No way."

"Yes, way. But the girls didn't want to teach her how to swim, did they Becka. No, they wanted to humiliate her. So they pushed her underwater. And every time she struggled and gasped, they would push her down again. And all the time they did this, the girls laughed and laughed and laughed."

Becka pleaded, "It was just a stupid prank. You were okay. You didn't drown. I saw you run away."

Marianne sneered.

The tide inside the cavern was rising. It had climbed up as high as Becka's knees and was rising steadily. She could feel the heavy sloshing of the water as the waves surged underground and erupted up into the cavern. "What are you going to do?"

Marianne appeared to have ignored her question. Her eyes lost all focus and seemed to draw inward toward some long-forgotten memory. "It's all right now, though. The little girl found a way to be friends with them after all."

"What are you talking about? What friends? Who are you?"

Becka frantically worked her way along the wall, fingers splayed against the barnacled rock, all the while the sea water continuing to rise. There must be a way out! The sea water was past her waist now.

"You're crazy," Becka screamed. "That's what you are! You ought to be locked up! I hate you! You hear me? I hate you!"

Marianne sighed. "That's no way to talk to your best friend, Becks."

"I'm not your friend," Becka snarled. Suddenly she felt something against her leg. She jumped sideways through the water. A hand reached around her ankle. It tightened and tried to pull her down!

"No!" Something coiled around her wrist. Frantic, she looked down. Another hand had emerged from the water. The fingers encircling her wrist were white as ivory and bloated as an inflated rubber glove. Becka screamed.

We're all here now, Becka.

Becka felt the breath leave her suddenly. Terror buckled her knees as another hand pushed up through the water. And another. And another. Bloated fingers reached for her. Clawed at her. She tried to dodge them, but it was no use. Suddenly an arm emerged from the water.

Becka tried to scream. But as the head of her best friend, Monica, bobbed to the surface—its features distorted like those of a hideous Halloween pumpkin—her words caught in her throat.

A second head rose from the depths. Becka felt the tears rolling down her face.

"Oh my," she whimpered. "Alicia!"

The sea water continued to rise. It climbed up just below Becka's neck.

Marianne sighed happily. "Don't worry, Becka. It won't hurt . . . much."

"You won't get away with this," sputtered Becka. The sea water was closing over her mouth. With her arms pinned to her sides she could not keep her head above water. Her friends were holding her down.

Marianne grinned.

"I told you I found a way we could all be friends."

When Marianne got back to the house she saw a very pretty girl standing impatiently on the front porch. "Who are you?" she asked.

The girl turned and gave Marianne a chilly once-over. "Isn't it a little early for Halloween?"

"I'm Becka's cousin, Marianne."

The girl cocked a hip. "Great. Where's Becka?"

Marianne turned and looked back over her shoulder, then at the girl. "You must be LizBeth."

The girl glared at Marianne. "Yeah. So? Where's Becka?"

"She and the rest of The Group are waiting for you down at Miller's Point."

"How do you know about The Group?"

Marianne smiled. "Oh, I know all about The Group." She gestured for LizBeth to follow.

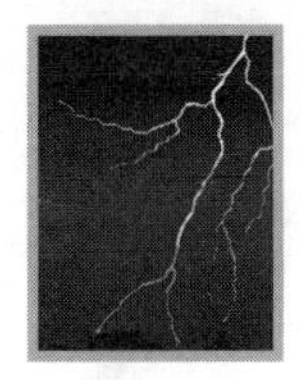

EMPTY EYES

Q. L. Pearce

The school board had planned for five years to build an Olympic-sized swimming pool for the students at Marshall High School. A crowd of students and teachers stood nearby to watch the excavation as the huge earth-moving machine took bite after tremendous bite out of the brick-red soil.

When the hole in the ground was finally uncovered, no one even noticed the dark oily shadow that oozed from the freshly opened hollow. The shadow soon blended with the shade under the trees on a nearby residential street. If anyone had seen it, they would have sensed that it was evil.

"Settle down, Lady!" Paul called from the family room to his frantically barking dog outside. Lady took no notice and continued to yelp and howl at the tabby cat she had treed in the backyard. Feigning indifference, the cat turned and began to tread gracefully along the branch. Suddenly it arched its back, laid its ears flat against its head, and hissed. There was something—something dark—among the leaves of the tree. Lady sensed it, too, and she began to whimper. As the cat exposed its sharp claws and slashed at whatever was threatening from the shadows, Lady scurried away with her tail between her legs, heading for the safety of the house.

"What's wrong, girl?" Paul asked his trembling dog as he opened the back door to let her in. She scrambled past him into the house and crept under the rolltop desk, where Paul had been doing his math homework.

"Looks like something gave her a scare," Paul's dad commented, walking into the family room. "I'm sure she'll be okay." He started to walk out of the room, then remembered why he had come in. "Hey, Son, I need a hand trimming the tree branches away from the side of the house, and restacking those packing crates of books in the basement. The way they're stacked now, I'm afraid they could fall and hurt somebody."

Paul closed his math book. "Sure, Dad," he answered. I could use a break from homework."

Moments later Paul was standing outside holding the end of a heavy rope that was tied around a thick tree branch. "When you feel the branch start to drop, give the rope a good tug so that it falls clear of the house," his father instructed from his perch at the top of the ladder.

"Okay," Paul said. His father steadied the handsaw and began to slice into the branch.

Suddenly a screeching, yowling cat leaped at his dad from the dense foliage of the tree. Its jet-black, oddly luminous eyes glittered wildly as it scratched ferociously at him. With a yelp of surprise, Paul's father teetered back and used the saw to fend off the hysterical creature. Grabbing the branch, he barely managed to keep his balance high atop the ladder.

The blow from the saw sent the cat sailing off the limb, and it landed with a thud on the ground. Paul rushed to the unconscious animal and ran his hand over its fur. "This is Pixie," he declared in astonishment. "She's Mrs. Kreska's cat. I can't believe it. She's usually so sweet. But did you see her eyes?"

"I can't believe a cat would take a fall that way," Paul's dad said when he reached the ground. "Cats always land on their feet, especially from such a short distance." He bent down and felt the animal's belly. "She's still breathing. I guess she just got spooked. Let's go inside and call Mrs. Kreska to come over and get Pixie. She'll be okay out here for a few minutes."

As Paul and his dad walked away, a dark shadow drained away from the stunned animal and formed a slick-looking pool on the ground. For a moment it remained still. Then it began to flow once again—toward the house. It slipped soundlessly into the small vent at the base of the chimney.

"It was so weird," Paul told his older brother, Steven. "She just jumped at dad out of nowhere like she wanted to rip him apart."

"That is weird," Steven agreed. "Maybe she'd eaten something that made her sick," he suggested. Then he turned up his lips in a slight smile. "Speaking of eating, Mom said it was okay if we had a couple of hot dogs for dinner tonight, and she said we could roast them over the fire in the den. We could even have marshmallows for dessert. How does that sound to you?"

"Cool!" Paul answered with a smile. "We can pretend we're camping out."

Paul looked forward to every other Saturday night. That was when his parents went out for the evening, and the two boys got to spend some time alone together watching TV or playing computer games. It was always fun. The brothers were very close, and Paul really looked up to Steven.

"You go get the hot dogs and skewers," Steven instructed. "I'll get the fire ready. I have to sweep out the ashes and set up the wood."

Paul ran off to the kitchen to get the food while Steven pushed aside the screen and reached inside the fireplace. Feeling around, he found the small lever that opened the flue and pushed it. As the metal cover opened with a squeal, something shadowy slithered across the smoke-darkened bricks of the fireplace and quickly covered Steven's hand like a dark evil stain.

"What in the world . . . ?" Steven withdrew his hand and rubbed it with the end of his T-shirt, but it didn't do any good. He rubbed harder, and the stain darkened. In the dim light it even seemed to glow slightly. Then the ebony pool started to slowly seep through the skin on his hands, then his wrists, and steadily moving up his arms

Scrambling to his feet, Steven rushed to the bathroom and turned on the hot-water tap full blast. Something very bizarre was happening to him. He couldn't seem to focus his eyes, and he felt as if something within his own body was squeezing him—wrapping itself around his mind like a predatory snake choking its helpless prey.

The steaming water was hot enough to scald him, but he plunged his hands under the stream, lathered them, and scrubbed hysterically. "Paul!" he screamed. "Help me!" A dark-veiled film began to close in over his eyes. "Stop it! It hurts!" he shrieked. "It hurts!"

Paul dropped everything, raced down the hall, and threw open the bathroom door. His brother was leaning over the sink. "Steven?" Paul cried. "What's the matter?" There was no answer. For a moment Steven didn't move. He just stood there taking deep, raspy breaths. Then, slowly, he turned to face Paul.

In his hand he held a sharp pair of hair-cutting scissors, but that wasn't what made Paul's pulse quicken. It was Steven's eyes. They were completely black and luminous, like polished spheres of obsidian. And they were vacant. Paul saw no sign of humanity in his brother's gaze.

"Steven—what's wrong with you?" Paul stammered.

But the thing that stood before him didn't answer. Instead, it uttered a low, gurgling growl and took a clumsy step toward him, lifting the glinting scissors high above its head. Paul backed away.

"Steven, this isn't funny. You're really scaring me." All at once, the thing bared its teeth and brought the scissors down in a deadly arc. Paul didn't hesitate. He darted from the bathroom and up the stairs, while the creature lumbered after him, snarling. Terrified, Paul made it to his room, slammed the door, and locked it. Behind him he heard the scissors stab deeply into the wood and snap.

Paul looked desperately from side to side for some sort of weapon. Then he decided it would be better to try to escape. This was crazy. That was his *brother* out there. What was the matter with him? Why was he . . . ? Then he remembered the cat . . . and its strange, dark eyes. He remembered how it had attacked his father, as if it had wanted to rip him to shreds.

"Why are you doing this, Steven?" he moaned softly. Paul didn't know what was happening, but he did know that he—and his brother—needed help.

Paul bolted to his window and pushed it open, even though he was already certain there was no easy escape there. His room was on the second floor and there was nothing to climb down onto. Once again he frantically looked around. Then, with shaking hands, he pulled the sheets from his bed.

"I can knot these together," he assured himself. "If I can just get next door to the Blakely house, I can . . ." He held his breath and listened. There was a metallic scraping noise at the door.

"It's got a key!" Paul gasped. Whatever was outside the door obviously knew the things that Steven knew—including where the ring of spare keys was kept. Now it was trying each key—one by one. Paul heard the sound of the correct key finally slipping awkwardly into the lock and slowly turning.

He dived under his bed as the door was flung open. It hit the wall with a loud bang. Paul barely breathed as he watched the thing step into the room. It shuffled slowly to the open window and looked out. Just then, Lady began barking and yapping in the yard below. *That's it, girl. Keep his attention*, Paul thought, realizing that the monster would eventually find him if he stayed where he was. He had to try to get out.

Paul's heart beat madly as he inched out from his hiding place, only a few feet from the terrible thing that had once been his brother. In slow motion he rose to his knees, then to his feet, and backed slowly—ever so slowly—toward the open door. He was shaking badly.

Just another second, he silently assured himself, then

eased through the door. But as he stepped onto the hardwood floor of the hallway, a single board creaked slightly under his weight. The thing at the window whirled around, and once again Paul stared into those horrible empty eyes.

In a flash, the creature lunged at him, and Paul took off. He had to make it down the stairs and to the front door. But at the bottom step, he felt himself lose his balance. Toppling forward, he fell hard on the landing. The thing leaped down at him, but Paul managed to roll out of the way. The monster that was Steven jumped to its feet and snarled. It had blocked his only escape to the outside. Paul made a move to one side. If he could just get to the kitchen, maybe he could—but the thing seemed to have guessed what he was planning. It took one step toward him, then another.

Thinking frantically, Paul realized that his only choice was the basement behind him. He barreled through the doorway and quickly locked himself in. Standing on the top step, he leaned against the wall, gasping for breath. Outside, the creature repeatedly threw its weight against the door, then abruptly stopped. Everything became quiet. Once again Paul heard the sound of a key being tried in the lock . . . then another. He had only a minute before the being, whatever it was, would open the door.

"What am I going to do?" he groaned under his breath. There was nowhere else to go. The only window in the basement was barred from the outside. It would only take seconds for the monster to find the right key. Paul looked around in panic. Then he saw something at the bottom of the stairs.

"The crates of books!" he whispered. They were stacked in three tall, unsteady columns.

A moment later the door to the basement swung open, and the thing in Steven's body stood silhouetted in the light from the entrance hall. Slowly it moved down to the first of a dozen steps. In his hiding place behind the stack of crates, Paul counted each step silently . . . *one, two, three, four*. He barely allowed himself to breathe . . . *five, six, seven, eight. Not yet . . . nine, ten. Not yet . . . eleven, twelve.*

NOW! his senses screamed, and he pushed outward with all his might. The stack of heavy wooden crates tipped and went careening down. The thing let out a single horrible cry, then lay still on the floor under a jumble of books and splintered wood.

Quickly Paul cleared away what he could and dragged his brother's limp body free. Steven's face was bleeding from a small cut, and there was a large bump developing on his head, but he was breathing regularly. Paul grabbed a coil of sturdy rope from a hook on the wall and began to securely tie his unconscious brother's hands and feet.

"I'm sorry I have to do this, Steven," he said in a choked voice. "I don't know what's happening here. But

I'm going to get you some help. I just don't want you to get loose until I do." He sat back and mopped the sweat from his forehead. "Mom and dad should be home soon and they'll know what to do. Hang in there, Steven. Hang in there."

In the darkened basement, Paul didn't see the oily evil shadow ooze from Steven's body and slip toward him.

Some time later Paul's mother and father arrived home. Paul was waiting for them at the front door.

"Paul?" his dad asked. "What are you doing up? I thought you'd be asleep by now. Where's Steven? . . . Paul, are you all right? . . . Paul?"

Clutching the scissors behind its back, the creature that had been Paul said nothing. He simply raised his head and stared at them with his black luminous eyes.

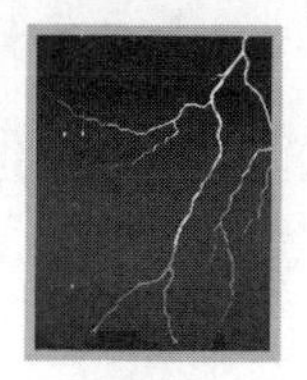

A "TRUE" STORY

R. C. Welch

Mark tossed the branch he had been playing with onto the fire. "All right," he said to the other students, "I've got one."

Mark and his classmates were on the annual Keystone Middle School's spring trip. This year the class had elected to go camping in the forested mountains of the Colorado Rockies. They had piled into a school bus early in the morning and had driven most of the day to reach the campground, now dotted with multicolored tent domes.

Although there were two teachers along for supervision, the boys who had been lucky enough to come were mostly left on their own. The teachers' tents were off to one side, far enough away to give the students the feeling of independence. Now, Mark and his buddies were taking advantage of their freedom by staying up long after the teachers had gone to bed and sitting around the campfire, trying to terrify each other with scary stories.

Kurt and Felix had already told some pretty petrifying ones, but Mark felt sure his would really rattle their wits. "I won't tell you how I heard about this," he began, his face eerily lit by the dancing flames of the fire, "but I will promise that what I'm about to tell you is a *true* story."

Kurt snorted, but was promptly hushed by the others. They had a "golden rule," which stated that each storyteller had to be given a fair chance, so Mark just ignored Kurt and began.

"There was this kid," he said in a hushed tone. "We'll call him Mike. He lived alone with his dad at the edge of town, real close to the forest where his dad worked as a lumberjack.

"Sometimes Mike's dad would be gone for a few days when he was working deep in the forest, so Mike learned how to take care of himself. He wasn't afraid of the woods like a lot of the other kids. In fact, he was always goofing around among the huge trees, setting traps and fishing and stuff. Pretty soon, he knew his way around the woods better than most anyone else.

"Anyway, one night while his dad was gone, Mike was sitting out on his front porch. He was staring up at the sky through his telescope when all of a sudden he saw a falling star. He watched it shoot across the sky, and then he realized he could track it with his telescope. He was following the fiery blaze, watching it fall closer and closer to earth, when it actually got close enough that he didn't need his scope anymore to see it. In fact, it was getting so near to him that he could feel the heat . . . especially since it was coming right at him!"

"Bam!" yelled Kurt, clapping his hands together sharply.

The boy sitting next to him jumped, and everyone else laughed and poked the poor guy in the ribs. Then Felix, the class science nerd, had to step in and ruin the mood.

"You know that's not really possible," Felix said. "Actually a shooting star is most likely to—"

"Fee-lix!" the other boys shouted him down. "Nobody wants a science lecture now."

"Are you guys through?" Mark said, pretending to be the adult in the group. He waited for everybody to settle down, then resumed his story.

"When Mike saw this thing flaming down out of the sky, he jumped for cover—and just in time. The meteor slammed into the ground about a hundred yards away. There was a huge flash of light and the sound of hundreds of trees snapping like pencils. Then everything got real quiet.

"Well, Mike didn't wait a single second. He took off running toward where he had seen the thing come down. But it was weird—there were no flames in sight. Still, it wasn't hard to find. All he had to do was follow the smell—not of fire, but of something like burning rubber.

"Within minutes, he reached the crash site. It was awesome. The trees were all smashed up like twigs, and in the middle of the clearing was this huge pile of dirt that had been pushed up like a wave. Smoke was coming from the dirt, and Mike decided to get closer for a better look at what he was sure was a meteor.

"Except it wasn't a meteor. It was something silvery that kind of glowed in the dark." Mark paused for a moment, then said practically in a whisper, "It was a spaceship."

Felix guffawed. "Yeah, right. And you said this was a *true* story."

Once again everyone chorused "Fee-lix!" until the bespectacled future scientist gave up and let Mark go on with his story.

"Well, needless to say, Mike couldn't believe what he saw," Mark began again. "So he slid down the pile of dirt until he was actually standing on the ship itself. The surface was shiny, smooth, and warm to the touch. Mike figured a lot of it was buried underground since it didn't look very big.

"Anyway, he was standing there, wondering what to do, when suddenly he heard a faint knocking sound. At first he thought it was the sound of the surface of the ship cooling, but then he realized that it was coming from *inside*. The knocking grew louder, and then—*Crack!*—a big gash opened up in the metal hull!"

Everybody flinched and the guy that Kurt had scared earlier gave a tiny yelp. The others teased him unmercifully, but Mark knew they were just trying to laugh off their own fright. He jumped up and started to walk around as he continued telling his story.

"The crack grew wider and wider until it made a circular hole. Then a horrible smell rolled out of the opening—it reminded Mike of the time he had found a rotting rabbit in a forgotten trap. It stunk so bad, Mike's legs went all rubbery, and he was shaking so much he could barely stand.

"Finally the crack stopped getting wider, so Mike inched his way closer to what was obviously some kind of doorway. His heart pounded so hard it practically made his shirt jump up and down, and the night seemed very quiet all of a sudden. He reached the edge of the opening and slowly leaned forward. Inch by inch, his head poked over the edge. He licked his lips, now dry with fear and excitement. He was going to be famous. He was going to be the first human ever to meet an alien!"

Mark looked around at his audience. He really had them, but knew he'd better get to the scary part soon. He went on, trying to make his voice sound ominous and spooky.

"First Mike saw some blinking lights on the inside wall. Next, he saw something that looked like a tunnel into the center of the ship. He leaned a little farther . . . and there it was—a dark shape lying in the middle of the tunnel.

"Suddenly a tentacle shot out! Before Mike could scream, it wrapped around his throat. He tried to get away, but the slimy thing was too strong for him. Gasping for breath, he felt himself being pulled over the edge of the hole and into the ship. The thing—a hideous cross between a spider and an octopus—had him . . . and it was pulling him closer to its mouth!"

Mark held his hands about a foot apart. "Mike was this close to going down the gross thing's ugly, slimy throat. In fact, he was so close he almost passed out from the stench of the thing's breath. Then its tongue—with millions of tiny teeth right on it—snaked out. It swirled across Mike's face like sandpaper, tearing into his cheeks and practically ripping off his nose. Then, just before he blacked out, Mike saw small tentacles ooze out of the alien's head. Although he tried, he couldn't fight off the alien as it sank one of its tentacles right into his skull and bored through it like it was a coconut, heading straight for his brain."

Mark paused while his audience made appropriate sounds of disgust. Then, before they had time to speak, he held up his hand.

"Wait a minute. There's more. You see, some time later Mike woke up. But he wasn't exactly *Mike* anymore. The alien had taken over, or assimilated, his body . . . *and* his life."

"What?" one of the boys gasped.

"That's right. Once it was comfortable in its new body, the alien set the ship to self-destruct. Then it followed Mike's memories back to the house where he had grown up. There it waited for its new human parent—Mike's dad—to return.

"And the worst part of the whole story is that poor Mike, even though he didn't have a body anymore, still had enough consciousness to know what was happening. He figured out that the alien would take over his dad, too; and that the more humans it assimilated, the more capable it was of reproducing itself over and over again. In time it would control the planet. And all Mike could do was watch in silent horror, knowing that he had brought about the doom of the human race."

Mark's voice dropped to a whisper as he finished, and he stood still in the flickering shadows cast by the waning campfire. The stunned silence was everything he could have hoped for. He waited as his classmates slowly began breathing again.

A boy named Malcolm sighed heavily. "It's like that movie where the scientists are at the South Pole and they find an alien that takes people over and makes copies of them." The boy shivered. "Afterward, the scientists couldn't tell who was real and who was a copy."

Kurt rolled his eyes. Of course *he* had to be the one to try to knock Mark's story down. Kurt was always the first to have something negative to say.

"I thought you said it was a true story," he accused. "That story was no more true than a fairy tale."

Mark looked at him innocently. "It *is* true."

Kurt shook his head. "Uh uh. No way."

Mark tried not to smile. Someone just had to figure it out. In fact, he had been betting on it. "Okay, smart guy," he challenged Kurt, "why is there no way it can be true?"

"There's no way because there was nobody around when the kid went into the spaceship," Kurt said, pouncing on what he was sure was the flaw in Mark's logic. "And if the kid never came out, and the alien blew up the ship, then there's nobody to tell the story and no evidence that the ship or the alien ever existed."

"That's true," Mark admitted. "But you missed one important point."

Everyone listened closely to see how he would defend himself.

"There *is* one person who knows the whole story," Mark said, nearly whispering, "but his name isn't Mike."

Suddenly Mark pulled open his shirt. "It's me!" he yelled as thick, black tentacles shot out from his chest.

Everyone screamed. It looked like a grenade had exploded in the middle of the circle as the boys jumped, crawled, or rolled backward away from the monster who had once been Mark.

"What is it?" yelled the teachers as they came racing over from their tents.

Mark knelt in front of the fire, nearly breathless with laughter. Tears streamed down his face as he propped himself with his hands to keep from falling over. The tentacles now bounced and swayed gently at his side, looking suspiciously like black nylons stuffed with something springy.

"What's going on?" demanded Mr. Owens, the English teacher.

Mark managed to catch his breath and tried to answer, but the sight of his classmates slowly picking themselves up made him break out laughing once again.

"Ah, nothing, Mr. Owens," said Mark's best friend, Zack, who had kept quiet throughout Mark's story.

"Nothing?" repeated Mr. DeRocha, the science teacher. "You were all screaming like it was the end of the world!"

Mark finally recovered enough to talk. "We were telling scary stories, and I guess mine was a little too scary."

The teachers—hands on hips—studied the group of kids. Everyone was trying to look as if it had been somebody else screaming and not them.

Finally Mr. Owens pronounced that it was late and that everyone had to be in their tents—*asleep*—within the next 15 minutes.

Most of the kids were still too embarrassed to do anything but agree. Some of them shot Mark dirty looks, but others grinned or gave him the thumbs-up sign, wishing they had been as clever as he was.

True to Mr. Owens's wishes, 15 minutes later everyone was in their tents, although not exactly asleep. The sound of whispered conversations and muffled laughter could be heard from every tent.

"Geez," Zack said in a low voice from his side of the dark tent he and Mark shared, "you nailed us all with that one."

Mark smiled. "You know, I think Nigel almost had a heart attack."

Zack clutched his chest and fell backward. The two boys burst into giggles and spent the next few minutes making jokes about who had been the most scared of the group.

After their laughing fit had passed, Zack asked Mark quietly, "Where did you get that story from, anyway?"

"Why?" Mark whispered.

"I mean, did you get it from that movie Malcolm was talking about?"

"What makes you think I made it up?" Mark asked, suddenly serious.

Zack was silent a moment. Then he said in an angry tone, "Come on, Mark. I really want to know where you got the story. Stop goofing around."

Mark didn't answer right away. The silence in the tent seemed to take on a life of its own. Finally the breath Mark had been holding in exploded out of his mouth in a bark of laughter. "Of course I made it up! What do you think—it really happened?"

There was a strange sound from Zack, as if his sleeping bag was being torn open. "Good," he sneered as he clamped a hand tightly over Mark's mouth. "I was worried for a moment that I'd been discovered."

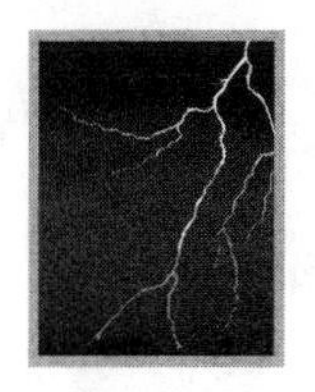

THE KEEPER OF THE WATCH

James Charbonneau

Billy kilmer was right behind Joe as the two boys entered the shop, a small bell tinkling their arrival. The shop was cramped and dark and Billy still didn't know what he was doing there. He had just done what he always did—follow Joe Grant wherever he went.

Billy wasn't really sure why he hung out with Joe in the first place. Maybe it was the way everyone always watched Joe walk through the halls in schoola study in cool. Or maybe it was the way Joe stood, with one foot cocked in front of the other, his hand resting loosely on his hip, his chiseled features always seeming to be in profile, while his other hand was reaching up and pushing back a shock of fine black hair from his forehead. Maybe it was just the way Joe refused to answer questions, not even when a teacher asked—*especially* when a teacher asked.

"What are we doing here, Joe?" Billy finally asked. "I've got to be home by—"

"Look, 1 have to do a stupid errand for my mom," Joe practically snarled. "I just thought you could help break up the boredom. But if you're gonna whine about having to get home, then just go."

"Wow, don't get all bent out of shape," Billy replied. "I just asked."

"Fine, then hang out for a minute," Joe said. "I'm supposed to pick up my mom's watch. The owner of this dump just fixed it."

While Joe went up to the counter, Billy checked out the shop. It was filled from one end to the other and from top to bottom, with clocks. Sitting in display cases and on counters and shelves were cuckoo clocks, alarm clocks, clocks shaped like hearts, twin black panthers with clocks in their bellies, digital clocks, clocks with hands in the shape of bird wings, airplane propellers, and even fingers. There on the floor stood grandfather clocks. Some so short Billy had to bend to see their faces, others so tall he had to lean back to take them all in. Billy whirled around in amazement. There were clocks of every kind in the crowded little shop—and they were all ticking, clicking, or whirring away.

The sound was almost overpowering, but Billy liked it. It reminded him of the pocket watch his grandfather used to let him wind when he was little.

"Be careful with it, boy," his grandfather used to say. "Old watches can't handle much pressure. They're extremely delicate and their insides will break if you wind them too tight."

"Hey, Kilmer! What're you doing?" Joe called. "Taking inventory of all this junk?"

Billy headed for the front of the store where joe still stood at the counter. "Junk?" Billy replied. "Mat are you, nuts?" He just couldn't believe some of the things Joe said sometimes. "Some of these clocks are really cool."

Suddenly an old man appeared behind the counter, causing both Joe and Billy to jump. "Can 1 help you?" he asked.

The two boys looked at each other. Neither of them had seen the man come out from the back room. It was as if he were gone one second, and then there the next.

Billy couldn't take his eyes off the man. It wasn't so much that he looked really old, but like the shop itself, he seemed to literally reek of age. He wore a long robe the color of black cherries and a black silk shirt that poked out from the collar. On the bridge of his nose sat an old pair of bifocals with a magnifying glass attached to one lens, making it impossible to see the man's eyes. And sticking out in all directions from his head was a wild mass of hair. To Billy, he looked like a cross between Einstein and some crazy wizard.

Joe just stood there staring at the man with his mouth open.

"Come, come boys," the man said, tapping the counter. "What do you need?"

"I, uh, I'm here to pick up my mom's watch," Joe finally said. "The name's Grant."

The old man smiled at Joe, then looked over his bifocals at Billy, but didn't say a word.

What's he looking at? Billy wondered, squirming uncomfortably. Then he took up Joe's defiant pose. But with Billy's rounded cheeks and freckles it didn't quite work, so he quickly turned away, hiding his flushed face from the man's gaze.

"Ah-h-h, yes! Mrs. Grant's watch," the old man said, shifting his attention back to Joe. "Your mother's spring was too tight."

"You're telling me," Joe said, with a nasty chuckle.

But the old man didn't even crack a smile. Instead, he slowly turned away from the counter and disappeared through a dark curtain.

While the man was gone, Joe wandered around the shop, and Billy, as usual, unconsciously followed him. In the center of the store stood a lone pedestal with a glass dome on top, and the two boys gravitated toward it. Whereas every other area of the place was jammed full, this one pedestal had nothing around it.

Both boys peered into the glass dome and gasped. Lying beneath the dome on a blue velvet pillow, was a pocket watch the likes of which neither boy had ever seen before. It was the same basic size and shape of most pocket watches, but this one was totally black except for its polished hands, which looked like tiny gold arrows. Where the numbers should have been, small, circular pictures took their place.

As Billy and Joe leaned in to get a better look, Billy saw that each of the pictures contained a frozen figure of a person in motion—one walking, one jumping, one skipping, one falling—something different for all 12 positions around the dial. As he stared at the magnificent timepiece, Billy could have sworn that the watch's face began to swirl, and for a moment he felt himself growing a little dizzy.

"Cool," Joe said in awe. "I've got to see this thing." But as he tried to lift the dome off the pedestal, he noticed that a small lock held it in place. He turned to Billy with a mischievous grin. "This thing's gotta be worth some major bucks," he whispered as if he were revealing some big secret.

"Yeah," Billy murmured. He'd never seen Joe so fascinated by anything. "It's probably worth at least—"

"Come away from there now, boys!" the old man suddenly called out, a little edge to his voice. "Young Mr. Grant, your mother's watch is ready."

As the boys moved toward the front counter, Billy was about to ask the old shopkeeper what kind of watch he had displayed under the glass dome, but Joe quickly jabbed him in the ribs, paid for his mother's watch, and headed for the door.

"Uh, see ya," Billy said, waving to the old man as he fell in behind Joe, who yanked the door so hard that the bell attached to the top nearly fell off.

"Yeah, so long," Joe called over his shoulder. Then he stepped out of the shop and whispered for Billy to hurry up.

"What did you jab me for?" Billy asked, once the door had closed behind them.

"I didn't want the old man to know we were interested in that watch," he said, looking into the shop over Billy's shoulder. When the old man disappeared behind the curtain, he grinned. "Quick, give me a boost."

"What do you mean?" Billy asked.

"Cup your hands, dummy!" Joe snapped.

Almost mechanically, Billy did as he was told. Then Joe boosted himself up, grabbed the bell off the shop's door, and jumped down.

"What did you do that for?" Billy asked, although he had a bad feeling he knew why.

"Never mind," Joe said, dismissing him with a wave. "Let's go."

Later that evening, Billy was upstairs in his bedroom doing his homework when he heard rocks bouncing off his window and someone calling his name.

He crossed over to the window, opened it, and looked out to find Joe standing there grinning up at him. "Get down here," Joe ordered.

"Why?" Billy asked. "I've got homework to do."

"You'll see," Joe replied mysteriously.

Curious, Billy climbed down the trellis under his window. He could at least find out what Joe wanted, right?

"Okay, I'm here," he told Joe, trying to sound cool and tough like Joe did. "But I'm not sneaking into any movies again. Last time we almost got caught, and I was afraid to go back to that theater for a month."

"We're not going to the movies," Joe said, rolling his eyes. "Just follow me. This is going to be good."

Angry with himself for giving in, Billy reluctantly followed Joe. When he found himself standing across the street from the clock shop, he got a sick feeling in his stomach. "Look, Joe," he began. "I don't know what you've got planned, but I don't—"

"I think the old man lives right in the shop," Joe interrupted as if whatever Billy said didn't matter. "I came back and watched him lock up." He pointed across the street to an upstairs window. "See that light up there? When it goes off, we can make our move."

Billy didn't need to ask what Joe had in mind. He just needed to figure out a way to get out of it.

"There's no alarm or anything," Joe went on with a snicker. "The old man just locked the door and headed straight upstairs."

Before Billy could say another word, he found himself being dragged across the street. As they got to the door of the shop, Joe looked anxiously up and down the sidewalk, and Billy found himself unconsciously doing the same thing. He was just about to protest, when Joe pulled a winter glove out of his pocket, put it on, and broke the small window in the door with his fist.

Billy's mouth just about hit the sidewalk. "I can't believe you really did that!" he gasped. "We've got to get outta here!"

But Joe already had his hand through the hole and was opening the door. "Keep a lookout," he whispered harshly as he stepped into the shop. "I'll be back before you know it."

Billy was so scared he didn't know whether to run or stay. He was just about to go into the store and pull Joe out, when he heard another crash—this one much louder. Then Joe appeared in the doorway breathing hard and smiling.

"Look at this!" he said excitedly as he showed Billy the black watch in the palm of his hand. "This thing is awesome!"

Just then, some lights went on in the back of the store. "Who's there?" called the old man. "Who's in my shop?"

"*Run!*" Joe yelled, taking off.

And, as always, Billy followed.

They raced down the street, panting and looking over their shoulders for about five blocks, then just near the entrance to the town mall, they stopped to catch their breath.

"I don't think anybody followed us,"Joe gasped.

"You've got to give that back," Billy said, between gulps of air.

"Oh yeah, after all that, that's exactly what I'm going to do," Joe replied sarcastically. Then he walked into the mall, laughing.

Billy ran after him. "I mean it, Joe," he pleaded. "You've got to take the watch back."

Ignoring Billy completely, Joe bought a soda at one of the food court stands, then sat down at a table to admire his prize. Wordlessly, Billy sank down into the scat across from him.

"This thing is so weird," Joe said, staring at the watch. He bounced it around in his palm. "It even *feels* weird."

His curiosity overwhelming him, Billy huddled over the stolen watch. At closer inspection, it was even stranger than it had appeared in its case. Not only did it seem to be moving, it also seemed to draw you into it. For a moment, the two boys just stared at it, until Billy finally shook his head as though forcing himself out of a trance. He looked at Joe who was still staring at it.

"Hey, Joe," Billy said. No response. "JOE!" Billy yelled, hitting Joe on the shoulder.

Shaking his head, Joe looked at Billy scornfully. "Hey, what are you hitting me for?" he snarled.

"Because you were going into La-La Land," Billy shot back immediately.

"Yeah, well this thing sort of draws you into it," Joe said defensively. Almost cautiously now he looked back at the watch. "Hey, what's this?" Joe gently touched a tiny button on the side of the watch as though he were afraid it might bite him.

Billy leaned over and looked at the tiny button. It was

right next to the stem used for winding the watch. "Looks like a stop watch button," he guessed. "I'd leave it alone. You might break—"

But before Billy could finish his sentence, Joe had pushed the button, and instantly both boys let out yelps of surprise as the whole world seemed to go into a tailspin. Grabbing each other as if they were both sliding into a whirlpool, they held on until everything came to a screeching halt.

"W—what was that?" Billy stammered.

But Joe didn't answer. He was too busy trying to comprehend what he was seeing.

There, all around them, the hustle and bustle of the shopping mall had frozen into stillness. People with arms full of packages and bags were stopped dead in their tracks. A woman bending down to scold her little boy was frozen, her finger in mid-wag. And her child's mouth, just opening to let out a wail, was locked solid in place. A large man, two tables down, was stiff as a board, his teeth biting into an overstuffed burrito, the contents of which hung in space as they fell toward the man's plate. And in one of the food court booths, a circle of pizza dough hung in mid-spin, three feet above the upraised fingertips of an unmoving pizza chef.

"Wow!" Billy cried. "What's going on?"

Joe spun around, trying to look in all directions at once, as he took it all in. Then he smiled slyly. "It's the watch," he said, feeling the timepiece literally pulsing in his palm.

Billy, still holding onto Joe's arm, realized Joe was right. He also realized that if he let go of Joe he'd probably freeze as well.

"You've got to hit the button again, Joe," he said evenly, trying to stay calm.

"Oh no I don't," Joe said with a sneer as he shoved Billy off of him—but not before Billy managed to punch in the button on the watch.

Wboosh! A white light nearly blinded Billy. When he finally could see again, he was on the floor, Joe was gone, and the mall had exploded back into activity. The people moved on with their packages; the woman went about scolding her son; the child released his wail; the man eating the burrito finished his bite; the contents of the burrito hit the plate; and the pizza spun back to the chef's hands. Several passersby looked at Billy sitting on the floor and wondered how he got there, but other than that, no one seemed to notice that a piece of their lives had been stolen away.

Suddenly, there was another blinding flash and Joe stood before Billy wearing an ear-to-ear grin. "Get up off the floor, Billy," he said. "You're attracting a crowd."

Billy scrambled to his feet. "Listen to me, Joe," he pleaded. "That watch is dangerous. You've got to give it back."

Joe shook his head. "Sorry, pal. This watch is mine now. And I'm going to have some fun with it."

"Then *I'll* have to take it back," Billy said, making a quick move toward Joe.

But the older boy easily stepped out of Billy's range. "Don't even think about it," he said. And with that, Joe let out a nasty laugh, turned, and quickly walked away.

In the weeks that followed, Billy didn't hang out with Joe much and strange things started happening around town. It started off with minor things. For instance, a teacher's chair vanished just as he was going to sit down, and a few kids found themselves standing in their underwear in the middle of the school hall. But then it got worse. First all the candy disappeared from Fineman's Pharmacy one afternoon. Then a bunch of video games were missing at Videorama. And finally all the money at the town bank vanished without a trace.

Billy knew what he had to do. And wearily one afternoon, he headed toward the watch shop.

"Hello, boy," the old man said the minute Billy entered the cluttered shop. "I've been waiting for you."

Billy didn't know what to do other than tell the truth, so he did.

"I'm Billy Kilmer," he began, "and my friend, uh, he stole your watch."

"I know," the shopkeeper said, as he continued to fiddle with the clock he was working on. He finally looked up and stared at Billy with eyes as black as midnight. Billy stepped back, afraid, and the old man quickly tried to reassure him with a warm smile.

"I knew the minute the watch was stolen because instantly I felt a burden lift off my shoulders," he went on, his eyes still fixed on Billy. "And yet, I still feel responsible. You see, many years ago, I stole the watch myself. And because of that one foolish act, I was forced to become, well, the keeper of the watch. It became my responsibility to protect the world from its power. Now it is no longer my burden—it is your friend's."

Billy swallowed hard. "But you don't understand," he told the man. "My friend, Joe—he'll use the power of the watch."

"Then it is up to you to stop your friend," the old man replied simply.

"*Me!*" Billy gasped. "Why me?"

"Because I am too old," the shopkeeper said. "You must be quick. You must get the watch from your friend before he can stop time again. And remember, while he is holding the watch, he can be invisible to you unless you maintain physical contact with him."

"I know," Billy mumbled dejectedly, remembering when Joe had vanished after he'd let go of his arm. "But what if I'm not fast enough?"

The old man leaned forward and grabbed Billy. "You *must* be fast enough," he said. "You must get the watch away from your friend and become the guardian of its power."

"No way!" Billy cried. "I don't want to be responsible for—"

But the old man had already turned and walked away toward the back room. "That watch was not meant to be on this Earth," he called over his shoulder, just before he disappeared behind the dark curtain.

Billy found Joe outside a store called Toy Universe. He had a wicked grin on his face and he was tossing the black watch up and down in his hand.

"Hi, Joe," Billy said as he casually walked up. "We need to talk."

Joe stopped tossing the watch and held it firmly in his hand. "Keep your distance, Billy," he warned. "I've got nothing to say to you, unless you want to help me trash this store."

Billy shook his head.

"Ah, you don't know how to have any fun, Billy," Joe said, turning away. "You're just a goody—"

In a burst of speed, Billy ran at Joe and locked him in a bear hug—but not before Joe managed to hit the button on the watch. Instantly the whole mall came to a silent halt, but because Billy still clung to Joe, he was not affected.

"Let go of me!" Joe yelled, wrenching out of Billy's grasp and knocking him to the floor.

But knowing that if he didn't stop Joe this time he'd never have another chance, Billy hung on and clung to Joe's ankle.

"I said, *let go*!" Joe shrieked, kicking his foot into Billy's stomach.

For a moment all the air left Billy's lungs, but he knew he had to hang on. And then he remembered what his grandfather had told him about winding watches too tight. "Listen to me, Joe," he gasped. "I talked to the old man and he said whatever you do, don't wind the watch too tight!"

"Why?" Joe demanded, looking down at Billy who was still clinging onto his ankle. And then Joe's eyes twinkled mischievously. "Oh, I get it! The tighter the watch is wound, the more powerful it becomes!" And with that he started turning the watch's stem. "I'll be the first teenager to rule the world!" he cried, winding the watch tighter and tighter.

But just before the last twist that would have broken it, the watch seemed to come alive. A black shadow grew out of its center, and in seconds, Joe was enveloped in darkness.

As Joe screamed in terror, Billy let go of his ankle. Then a flash of light filled the air, and everything in the mall burst back into motion again . . . except Joe.

Scrambling to his feet, Billy walked over to what looked like a statue of his friend. Joe's face was locked in a terror-filled stare, and in his frozen hand, he still held onto the watch—barely. For at that very instant, the ancient timepiece was beginning to slip from his rigid fingers.

Seeing this, Billy dove to catch the watch . . . and it landed in his palm just inches from the hard marble floor. Sighing with relief, Billy stood up and looked into Joe's unseeing eyes. Then, in one last desperate attempt to break the watch's horrible spell, Billy flung it to the floor with all his might . . . but the watch remained completely unharmed.

Dazed, Billy picked up the watch and held it in his closed palm. Joe was clearly doomed, but in a way, so was he. For now Billy knew the awful truth. He was the guardian of the watch, responsible for keeping it away from others, responsible for not succumbing to its powers himself.

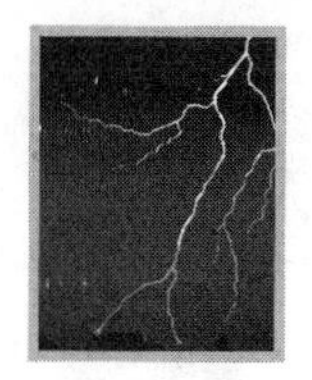

TOMBSTONE BLOOMS

Scott Ingram

Jeremy's pale pink tongue made a landing pad for snowflakes as he spun slowly beneath the February sky. Wind shrieked low and angry across the valley. Icy crystals whipped around his neon green parka and dark blue snowpants.

"Jeremy Miles, what are you doing?" Becky didn't want to sound impatient, but sometimes Jeremy could be so pokey. It was freezing, and if he caught cold, Mrs. Miles would blame her.

"I'm trying to swallow snowflakes," Jeremy answered, reeling in his tongue and dizzily stopping to look up at his baby-sitter. "But it's too windy to catch them." He galloped along the sidewalk in front of her, an eight-year-old bundle of freckles, energy, and curiosity.

"I knew that," said Becky. "But isn't it tough to spin around and hold your head up? If I tried it, I'd fall flat on my behind."

Becky smiled. She enjoyed the long walks with Jeremy. Mrs. Miles was her new neighbor—and the new town librarian. Becky's father, James Warren, was president of the library board, and he'd made the decision to hire her.

When Mrs. Miles mentioned that she needed after-school help for Jeremy, things fell into place for Becky and suddenly she had a job.

It was a fun job, too. Jeremy liked to go out exploring the narrow streets and quaint houses of his new town every afternoon, and Becky loved showing him around. The Warren family had lived in Penfield since the early 1800s; the town—its streets, its houses, and most of its stories—were like a family album for Becky.

Jeremy stopped galloping a few feet ahead of Becky and began to spin again, this time like the wobbly top he kept in his wooden toy chest. He spun until his legs gave out and he fell flat on his back—*crump*—in the gathering snow.

"Owww! Owww!" Jeremy yelped, grabbing the back of his head and twisting in pain. As he rolled from the spot where he had fallen, Becky saw the dark shape of a stone pushing through the blanket of snow.

"Jeremy! Are you okay?" Becky asked in a panicky voice. She was worried about him, but was even more worried about what Mrs. Miles would say if Jeremy was badly hurt. Mrs. Miles was extremely protective of her son.

"I bumped my head," Jeremy said, fighting back tears. "Stupid rock!"

Becky lifted off Jeremy's knitted cap and gently rubbed the knot that had risen through his sandy blond hair. Just a bump, she thought. *Lucky. This kid is so bouncy, it's amazing he doesn't have bumps and bruises all over him.*

"Come on, pal," Becky said, lifting up Jeremy and brushing him off. "The snow is really coming down and it's getting dark. Your mom is probably back from the library already. Let's take a shortcut."

"Shortcut?" Jeremy said eagerly. "Where?"

"Through the old cemetery on the hill," Becky answered, pointing toward a rising slope behind a bent, rusting, wrought-iron fence. "The other side of the hill comes down almost in your backyard."

Jeremy hesitated.

"You're not really afraid, are you?" Becky asked. Then, breaking into a smile, she coaxed, "Come on. It'll be fun. There's some really neat tombstones to look at."

The gravestones were shadowy silhouettes against the snowy curtain as the eighth-grade baby-sitter and her younger companion crunched and squeaked through the powdery snow. Jeremy clung tightly to Becky's hand, partly to keep from slipping, but mostly because he'd never walked through this spooky place before. The little boy's giant imagination overflowed with laughing skulls and rotting corpses.

"Hey, Becky!" Jeremy said excitedly, tugging at Becky's mittened hand. "What're those purple flowers over there?"

Becky's eyes followed Jeremy's pointed finger to a small, weathered gravestone a few feet away. There, almost covered by blowing drifts, was a bouquet of violets, weighted down against the wind.

"Flowers?" Becky wondered out loud. "This time of year?"

The twosome held hands as they slid a short way to the wind-worn grave marker that stood apart from other family burial plots. Becky knelt close and looked at the flowers.

"I knew they couldn't be real," she said, as Jeremy leaned close to her, his nose dripping like a faucet. "They're silk violets, Jeremy. See? Pretty, aren't they?"

"Yeah," he said in a hushed voice. "Who's buried here?"

Becky brushed away the layers of snow that had packed against the cracks of the old stone. With her finger, she traced the letters and numbers cut into the stone slab:

JEFFREY 1850–1858

Becky looked down at Jeremy. "No last name," she murmured. "That's strange."

Jeremy looked uncomfortable. "He was only eight when he died. The same age as me."

"Right," Becky said, shivering from a chill she knew had not been caused by the biting wind. "But he died almost a 140 years ago. I wonder who left—"

"Come on, Becky. Let's go," Jeremy said, pulling impatiently on her sleeve. "I wanna get home and watch cartoons."

By the time Becky and Jeremy arrived in the Miles's backyard, darkness had slid over the town. The square eyes of lighted windows blinked in the new homes of the Penfield Acres subdivision. Becky could tell from the glow in the kitchen window that Mrs. Miles was already home from work. *She's probably worried,* Becky thought. *We should have been here sooner.*

"There you are!" Mrs. Miles tried to sound welcoming, but the edge in her voice and her paler-than-usual face revealed her concern. "I was afraid you'd lost your way in the storm." She looked hard at Becky through the thick lenses of her gold-rimmed glasses as she knelt to help Jeremy remove his snowy outer layers of clothing.

"Mom! Guess what we did?" Jeremy began. "We cut through—"

"What happened!" Mrs. Miles had felt the bump on Jeremy's head when she took off his hat. She whirled toward Becky. "How did he get this bump?"

Becky was so startled by the fury of Mrs. Miles's question that she could hardly speak. "He—he was spinning around, and . . . and he fell."

"Stupid rock!" said Jeremy, seemingly unaware of the tension between his mother and his baby-sitter.

Mrs. Miles stood and rubbed her temples. *In her ruffled silk blouse, long skirt, and high-button shoes. Mrs. Miles looked more like Jeremy's great-grandmother than his mother*, Becky thought.

"Jeremy, why don't you go to your room and watch your television program," Mrs. Miles said, smiling sweetly at Jeremy as he scooted into the living room. She turned back to Becky. "I—I'm sorry, Becky. I didn't mean to snap at you. It's just that I worry so about Jeremy. You know how spirited he is—and accidents, well, they happen to children his age."

"I'm sorry, too. Mrs. Miles." said Becky. "He just stumbled so quickly. And who knew there would be a rock?"

"Of course. Who knew?" Mrs. Miles whispered. She sighed deeply and pushed a wisp of gray hair back into the bun held in place by her embroidered hairband. "I just hope that you'll be more attentive to the trouble an eight-year-old can get into."

"Okay, Mrs. Miles," Becky said, looking at the floor. "See you tomorrow."

Becky had only a short walk across the street to her house, but the howling wind battled her every inch of the way. As she turned away from a particularly strong blast, her gaze fell on the Miles's house. Mrs. Miles stood at the window of the den a moment before pulling her curtains shut. *She sure seems old to have a kid as young as Jeremy,* Becky thought, turning toward home.

Dinner was waiting when Becky finally walked into her warm kitchen. She could smell the soup's steamy welcome the minute she sat down at the table, and she quickly forgot the odd end to the afternoon.

"How was your time with Jeremy, Becky?" her mother asked as she ladled thick chowder into a bowl. "Did he wear you out as usual?"

"No, he froze me out," Becky said, blowing on her soup. "We must have been outside for three hours. I'll tell you, in the two months I've been watching that kid, we must have walked a zillion miles around this town."

Mrs. Warren smiled at her daughter. "I'm surprised you went outside today. Didn't you tell me Mrs. Miles was afraid Jeremy might catch a cold?"

"Yeah. But she's afraid of *everything*. I didn't see any harm in taking Jeremy for a walk—even if it was snowing." Becky buttered a thick slice of pumpernickel bread and took a big bite. "He's a really active kid," she went on, her mouth full. "He can't stay cooped up just because it's a little cold outside. I just wish . . . oh, forget it."

Mr. Warren eyed Becky. "What's wrong, sweetheart?" he asked. "You seem edgy. Aren't you enjoying your baby-sitting job?"

"It's just that Mrs. Miles freaks out if Jeremy gets the tiniest little scratch," said Becky. "It's like she doesn't want him to be a kid. She wants him to sit still like a doll or a statue or something."

"Well . . . some parents are very protective, Becky," her dad said. "Mrs. Miles is older. She's a single parent. Maybe having a rough-and-tumble boy like Jeremy is too much for her."

Becky smirked. "He is a handful, that's for sure. And she's just so . . . so spooky. It's like she's from some other time, you know?"

Mrs. Warren nodded. "Dad said she seemed old fashioned, but she had good references from her job up in North Cornwall. She was willing to work for the pitiful salary Penfield offered."

"Well, they bought a house so she must have some money," Becky said, who had become very aware of money now that she had a job. "Jeremy has nice clothes," she added. "And I think she makes some of them."

"I'll bet Mrs. Miles makes extra money as a seamstress. She's really talented," Mrs. Warren said, finishing her soup. "She sewed pillows for the children's reading corner in the library that are elegant—lavender silk. Too bad they'll have little greasy handprints on them in a matter of days."

Becky looked up from her soup. She thought of the unique, delicate clothes Mrs. Miles wore. The beautiful lace curtains. The dainty hairband. And . . . "Lavender? You mean, like, violet?"

"Yes. Why?" her mom asked.

"No reason, Becky said, finishing her soup.

"I can't find my train anywhere," Jeremy said, walking slowly into the Miles's kitchen where Becky sat doing her homework.

"You have an electric train set?" Becky asked, closing her book. Jeremy wasn't feeling well today, she could tell. His face was pale and there were dark circles beneath his eyes. There was no sparkle there anymore.

Lately, he'd seemed almost too tired to stand up. His voice sounded weary and close to tears. Maybe it was the dreary gray days of late March that drained the energy from him, but he wasn't the same bundle of energy she had known in the first few months.

"No. Not electric. Wood," Jeremy said, plopping down heavily in the chair next to Becky. "All my toys are wood. Mom says my dad was good at making stuff."

"Your dad?" Becky asked, surprised. Jeremy had never mentioned his father before. In fact, since Mrs. Miles looked so old, and Jeremy was so young, Becky had wondered whether—

"Not my *real* dad. I don't know my real dad. I'm adopted," Jeremy said matter-of-factly. "The dad that made wooden stuff was married to my mom. He died. I don't remember him."

Becky wanted to change the subject. Something about it was making her feel she was prying into business that wasn't hers. "Well, let's see if we can find your train," she said. "Have you checked everywhere in your room?"

Jeremy nodded. "Yup. And I can't find my top either. Or the stuffed horse my mom sewed."

"How about in the living room?" Becky asked.

Jeremy nodded. "I looked there. And the basement."

"Well . . . let's look in the den," Becky suggested.

Jeremy shook his head. "Mom doesn't like me to go into the den. I might mess stuff up."

Becky thought that was kind of odd. "Well, can we stand in the doorway and look from there?" she asked.

Jeremy grinned weakly. "Sure."

The french doors leading to the den were closed. Thick drapes covered the glass panes. It appeared to Becky as though Mrs. Miles definitely wanted to keep the room private. But as tired as Jeremy was acting, his old curiosity and his desire to find his missing toys gave him an extra burst of energy. He pushed open the doors.

In the dim afternoon light, the room seemed to be a place from a time long ago. Mrs. Miles's sewing machine was a wooden antique with wrought-iron legs and a foot treadle. The rug was worn, but its faded flower pattern reminded Becky of rugs in her grandmother's house. There was a musty attic smell that Becky thought might come from the stacks of old, leather-bound books scattered around the room. There was so much clutter—books, fabric, papers—that finding any toys would be impossible unless she went in and lifted things up.

Becky heard footsteps coming up the porch. *Mrs. Miles!* she thought, looking at Jeremy, who obviously thought the same thing. Quickly, Becky pulled the den doors shut behind them as the front door squeaked open. As she did, her eye was caught by the ornate gold lettering on a book that lay on an old desk. She couldn't make out the whole title. All she could read in a split second while she was hurrying from the room was *Spells and Incantations*.

Becky and Jeremy were sitting at the kitchen table by the time Mrs. Miles had taken off her coat and hung it in the front hallway. She appeared in the doorway with a tense expression lining her face.

"Hello, Becky," she said through chattering teeth. "Hello, Jeremy, darling. How are you feeling?"

Water dripped from the ends of her hair. *How could she have gotten so wet in the short walk from the bus stop at the corner to the house?* Becky wondered. Then she noticed the mud on the edge of Mrs. Miles's long skirt—and over the tops of her high-button shoes. It seemed odd—especially since the way home was all sidewalk.

"Jeremy seems tired, Mrs. Miles," Becky said, trying to ignore the shiver of fear creeping up her spine. "He just hasn't been himself for the past few days."

Mrs. Miles said nothing as she walked to the kitchen sink and began washing her hands. Becky saw that they, too, were muddy. *Did she fall on the way home?* Becky's mind raced. *And why isnt she saying anything about it?*

"Poor Jeremy," Mrs. Miles said over her shoulder. "He's been awakened by terrible dreams lately."

"They're scary," Jeremy said. "I don't remember them exactly—something was grabbing my arm. A monster, sort of. But it doesn't growl, it makes noises like—like a big machine."

"He's had difficulty falling back to sleep," Mrs. Miles continued. "I rub his back and try to soothe him." She paused and flicked the water off her hands. "Perhaps he's watching too much television. What an infernal device."

Becky forced a smile at the old-fashioned words. As Mrs. Miles shut off the water and turned back to the table, Becky noticed dark circles under the older woman's eyes. Her hands were trembling as she dried them. Her skin was so pale it looked almost bloodless. Becky remembered an old expression of her grandmother's: *Like death warmed over*.

"Well, I imagine your mother and dad will be expecting you, dear," Mrs. Miles said in a brittle voice. "I won't be needing you tomorrow."

Becky looked up from buttoning her coat. She had watched Jeremy every day for three months. "Is—is something wrong?"

"No. Jeremy has an appointment, that's all." She smiled and the skin stretched tightly against the corners of her mouth. "Come, dear," she said, stroking the back of Jeremy's head. "Let's wash up for supper."

"Okay, well, I hope the doctor can help," Becky said as she snapped her raincoat.

"Doctor?" Mrs. Miles looked puzzled.

Jeremy looked frightened. "I don't wanna go to the doctor, Mom!"

"You—you said Jeremy had an appointment, right?" Becky asked.

"Yes, Mrs. Miles said in a cold voice. "But it's *not* with a doctor. Good-bye, Becky. I'm sure your parents are expecting you."

Becky walked home through the misty rain, fighting a strange fear that she could not name. The good-bye had sounded so final.

Becky was lost without Jeremy the next afternoon. To kill time, she walked home from school instead of taking the bus. She wandered slowly through Penfield, trying to force the image of the tired, pale boy out of her mind and replace it with memories of the happy, sandy-haired boy who had become such a large part of her life in a few short months. Finally, in her aimless wandering, Becky found herself outside the broken-down gates of the old cemetery. She had a sudden urge to go to the gravestone she'd discovered with Jeremy on their snowy walk.

The thawing ground was slick as Becky made her way up the slope. She was certain the violets would be faded and worn by now. It had been a long winter and the rain over the past few weeks had fallen in buckets.

Becky made her slippery way to the forlorn stone that gave only the first name of child whose life had ended after eight short years. As she drew closer in the dim gray light, she was struck by a bolt of fear. Her eyes grew wide as a thought suddenly came to her.

The violets! They look brand-new! Becky's mind raced through the possible explanations as she knelt to study the handmade flowers. As she picked up the bouquet she noticed a small mound of freshly dug soil. Fighting against her instinct to run away, she began to claw at the mucky dirt. It took only a few swiping motions until she felt something hard. She dug deeper and pulled out a wooden train. A few more frantic gouges uncovered a top and a stuffed, handsewn horse.

The Miles's house was dark, except for a dim light in the den, as Becky ran into their backyard. She sprinted through their gate and across the street to home. She dashed in the front door, gasping for air.

"Mom! Mom! Is dad here?"

"Becky! What's wrong, dear?" asked Mrs. Warren.

"There—there's something weird . . . something really weird about Mrs. Miles," she said, trying to keep her body from shuddering. "I think Jeremy might be in trouble!"

"Now, Becky, I know Mrs. Miles seems a little eccentric. But don't let your imagination get the better of you," Mrs. Warren said, trying not to let the terror in Becky's eyes affect her. "Your father is in the den. But why—"

Becky dashed down the hall to the den. Mr. Warren was sitting at his word processor, working on the library annual report. He whirled around in his swivel chair when Becky banged through the door without knocking.

"Becky, you know I've asked you not to—"

"Sorry, Dad. But this won't wait," Becky said, running over to the bookshelves. Mr. Warren was very proud of his large collection of old books.

"Where do you keep your history books?" Becky asked as she ran her finger over the gold-lettered titles.

"Well, that depends," Mr. Warren said, pleasantly surprised by his daughter's sudden interest in his collection. "Which era are you interested in learning about? I have an excellent series on—"

"Penfield. Do you have a history of our town from around 1860?" Becky asked impatiently.

Mr. Warren walked over to the shelf and pulled down a thick volume titled *Penfield 1800–1865*. Becky grabbed the book from his hand and frantically flipped the pages. She stopped suddenly at a pen-and-ink sketch of a large brick factory building. The caption read: *The Mills Door and Window Company was one of the largest employers in the Penfield River Valley during the 1850s.*

"Mills Door and Window," Becky said softly. "That must have been a woodworking factory." She read down the page.

"One of the biggest," Mr. Warren said. "Or so I've read. The building burned down around 1900. But it was closed for years before that. Sometime in the late 1850s, I think."

"Why did it close?" Becky asked.

Mr. Warren knit his eyebrows, trying to recall the facts. "I'm not sure. Something about a death—maybe the owner or—"

"Or the owner's son!" Becky pointed excitedly to a paragraph in the old book. "It says that the owner's son, Jeffrey, an eight-year-old boy, was playing at the factory one day. The loose sleeve of his shirt caught in a machine. The boy was pulled into the machine and crushed to death." Becky read a few paragraphs more, then dropped the book on the floor and turned to her father with a look of terror.

"What's wrong, Becky?" Mr. Warren asked.

"Dad . . . the boy who was killed. His name was Jeffrey. Jeffrey Mills. He died in March—this time of year. He was buried in the old cemetery. The family closed the shop and moved—to North Cornwall!"

"Yes . . . so?"

"So, isn't that where Mrs. Miles is from?" Becky asked.

"Yes, she said she had been in that town for many years."

"And isn't her son—adopted son—named Jeremy?"

"Yes . . . Becky, I'm afraid I don't understand what all this is about," Mr. Warren said. Now it was his turn to be impatient.

"Jeffrey Mills . . . *Jeremy* Miles," Becky said. "They're almost the same . . ."

"But Becky, the Mills boy died almost 140 years ago," Mr. Warren said. "And Jeremy is a rambunctious little boy across the street."

Becky walked to the window and pulled back the curtain. She looked across the street to the Miles's house. The only light came from the window in the den. She turned and looked at her father, tears welling in her eyes.

"I'm afraid for Jeremy, Dad," she said, choking back a sob.

Becky couldn't sleep. All she could think about was the buried toys she had uncovered. The wooden toys. The woodworking factory. *Jeffrey Mills . . . Jeremy Miles . . .* The names ran through her mind as raindrops pattered against her window. Then Jeremy's words in describing his dream came to her: *something was grabbing my arm . . . like a machine . . .*

Becky threw off the covers and got dressed. The clock read 3:58. She grabbed a flashlight, threw on her raincoat, and slipped quietly out the front door. The only sound as she crossed the street was the squeak of her rubber boots and the drumming of the rain.

The light was still on in the Miles's den as Becky walked slowly along the front porch. The curtains were parted slightly; when she looked in the window, the room was empty. The door to the den was open and Becky could see the violet glow of a fluorescent light in the kitchen.

Becky decided to sneak around to the back door to get

a closer look into the kitchen. She stepped lightly off the porch and crept around the side of the house. The rain was coming down harder, and the soft ground sucked at her boots, almost pulling them off with each step.

As she turned the corner into the backyard, she froze. The floodlight was on. The back door was open. Becky shined her light across the yard. The beam fell on a set of footprints about the size of her foot. She walked over for a closer look. The prints sunk deep into the muddy ground, much deeper than her own feet were sunk. It was almost as though the person who made them had been carrying something. Or someone.

Jeremy! Becky clomped up the back steps and into the kitchen. She was past caring whether Mrs. Miles would yell at her or call the police. All she cared about was Jeremy.

"Jeremy! Jeremy!" Becky shouted as she ran through the rooms. Something was terribly wrong. The house was empty. Finally, Becky came to the den and burst in. There, on the same table where she had seen it, was the old book—*Spells and Incantations*. It was open to a page near the center. Becky put her hand over her mouth and sobbed as she read:

An eye for an eye, a life for a death,
The Master of Darkness accepts.
One to replace the one who resumes,
A body flawless, save only the wounds

Mark ye the date, prepare for the grave . . .
Give up the other for the one ye would save.

"Jeremy! Jeremy!" Becky's screams were swallowed by the driving rain as she ran through the backyard toward the cemetery. The flashlight beam bounced against the black curtain of night as she struggled up the mucky rise.

"Jeremy!" Becky screeched as she came over the hill and shined her light down the slope toward the lonely grave. Her body quivered as she moved closer. The mound was larger than it had been in the afternoon. Large enough to cover an eight-year-old . . .

Hard rain pounded the mucky spot as Becky shone her light. The yellow beam moved across the gravestone, and Becky's eyes grew wide as she looked closely at the letters cut into the stone.

JEREMY 1850–1858

"Jeremy!" Becky cried, but she knew Jeremy would never hear her again. She stood and swung her flashlight across the dark ground. Suddenly she stopped the beam. Footprints leading out of the cemetery disappeared into the darkness. Two pair. One was about the size of a woman's foot, the other the size of a child's. They were side-by-side, close together, moving in the same direction. Becky looked back at the tombstone. On the ground was a fresh bouquet of silk violets.

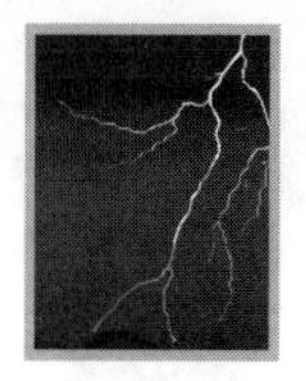

THE CRISPY HAND

Mark Kehl

Rich and Tommy had heard the tale a million times—every time they visited their grandmother. When they were younger, it used to keep them up at night. But Tommy was 12 now, Rich 14, and they were tired of hearing about the Crispy Hand.

However, the story was a tradition and unavoidable. So after an excellent dinner of ham and Grandma's secret-recipe mashed potatoes, and after Rich and Tommy had done the dishes, the boys gathered in the living room, where their mother and grandmother were drinking tea.

"Tommy, would you throw another log on the fire, please?" his grandmother asked. She gave him a sinister smile. "You'll want all the light you can get after you hear the story of . . . the Crispy Hand!"

Tommy restrained himself from rolling his eyes as he moved to the wood bin. He fed the fire a split chunk of oak and then sat on the hearth to enjoy the heat. Rich sat with their mother on the sofa. Grandma was in her chair close to the fire, an afghan wrapped around her legs. She held her teacup and saucer in her lap, where they occasionally rattled from her trembling.

"A long, long time ago," she began, "something bad happened in this very town."

Rich mouthed the words along with her. Tommy had to put his hand over his own mouth to keep from laughing. Their mom knew how tired they were of this story—they had complained about it all afternoon during the car ride—but she had told them to show respect for their grandmother and to listen. Their mom nudged Rich to make him stop, and Tommy focused on Grandma so he wouldn't be tempted to laugh by watching any further antics of his brother.

"Before I was born, when most of the land around town was still forest, the townspeople were very suspicious of outsiders. Back then, people didn't travel as much as they do today. You didn't just hop into your car and drive four hours to see your grandma. You saw more horses on the road than automobiles, and there were no airplanes. Our town was 10 miles from the nearest railroad line. So not too many strangers passed through these parts, and when they did the townsfolk made good and sure to find out their business and keep an eye on them."

Tommy risked a glance at Rich, but he was behaving himself now, becoming engrossed in the story despite himself.

"One day, as dusk was thickening into night, the town constable got word that there was a stranger walking on the forest road toward town. A farmer heading into town had spotted the man, large and hairy like a bear, and word spread through the small town like wildfire. So the constable and his deputies rode out to meet this stranger. The constable rode a fine chestnut mare. The two deputies followed with the police wagon hitched to a team.

"They had no problem finding the stranger. He was walking along the side of the road, just as they'd been told. However, he wasn't the bear of a man they expected. He was tall, yes, but his big coat hung on him as if he were made of broomsticks. His dark hair hadn't been cut in a long time. Between it and his thick facial hair, he *did* look a lot like an animal. But not a fierce one—just a tired and hungry one.

"The constable pulled up in front of the man. Letting the stranger get a good look at his rifle, he asked his name and his business. The stranger stared wearily and then shook his head. The constable raised his voice and asked again. The stranger held out his empty hands and in a deep, rough voice said something in a language the constable did not understand. Neither did his deputies.

"So the constable ordered his deputies to lock up the man in the police wagon. The stranger didn't understand as they stepped warily toward him, but when they tried to grab him he struggled fiercely. However, he was no match for the two strong deputies, and they locked him in the police wagon.

"'We'll let him spend a night in jail,' the constable said. 'Tomorrow we'll let him loose a few miles up the Barnesville Road. That'll let him know his kind ain't welcome here.'"

"The deputies knew this routine well—that's what they did with any stranger who came to their town without a darn good reason. So they drove the wagon back to the jail, which in those days was an old timber building that had been around longer than any other building in town. They used to say that the rebels locked up British loyalists there during the Revolutionary War. It was a squat building made of rough-hewn logs that had turned black with age, and it had crude iron bars over the windows. It was old, but it did the job. Kind of like me."

Tommy and the others smiled at the familiar joke.

"The deputies did as they were told. They took the stranger to jail and locked him up, the only prisoner there."

Grandma paused to sip her tea. *What a horrible place to stop*, Tommy thought, knowing what came next and wishing she would get it over with. Grandma took a second sip of tea and then resumed the story.

"No one knows how the fire started, but in a wooden building of that age it came as no surprise. It was cold that time of year, and the heat came from an old coal stove. Maybe a stray ember landed on the roof, or maybe a bird had made a nest in the chimney, or maybe one of the deputies had been careless with the stove door, allowing a

spark to jump out. The cells were full of
oners to sleep on. That straw made good tinder, an
you knew it, that old wooden jail was one big bonfire.

"As soon as someone spotted the fire, they rang the church bell. In those days, everybody in town dropped whatever they were doing and came to fight a fire. There were no hydrants or fire trucks, so they had to use buckets. They formed long lines stretching from well pumps to the fire. Then they passed the full buckets along the line and the empty ones back. Not the best way to fight a fire, but the best they could do.

"They tried to save the jail, but it just burned too fast. Even with four lines feeding buckets of water, it was like spitting on a campfire. But they tried, and all the while the townspeople could hear the strange foreign shouts of the stranger in his cell.

"Finally, the heat became too fierce, and they couldn't get close enough to throw their buckets of water on the flames. It was a lost cause, and they all knew it. Somberly, they watched the jail burn. From one window, a hand reached through the bars, grasping at life and freedom. Its fingers clutched and strained as the horrified people watched. Strange foreign screams rose from the heart of the blaze."

Tommy decided he was warm enough and moved away from the fireplace to sit on the sofa with Rich and his mom.

"The next morning the jail was nothing more than smoking ash and cinders," Grandma continued. "The constable and his deputies sifted through it but found no sign of their prisoner, not even the hand that had tried so hard to reach freedom. With nothing to bury, they shrugged and started to clean up the mess. They had a new jail to think about. They forgot all about the stranger whom they had, in a manner of speaking, murdered.

"That night, as one of the deputies lay in his bed, he heard something. He lived by himself and had no pets, but he could tell something was in the house with him. He heard a soft scuffling across the bare wood floor. *Mice*, he thought. Tomorrow, he told himself, he would get some traps. But tomorrow would never come for him, for a few moments later something locked around his throat. The thing seemed thin and brittle, but its grip was superhumanly strong. The deputy could not breathe. He tried to pry the thing free, but it clung too tightly.

"The constable found his body the next day when the deputy didn't show up for work. He was in bed, with the sheets and blankets all thrown about. His bloodshot eyes bulged from his face, and his bloated tongue protruded from his mouth. The oddest thing was what showed on his bruised neck: a set of sooty marks that looked as if they'd been made by the fingers of one hand."

Tommy found himself rubbing his neck, imagining the feel of charred fingers digging into the soft flesh.

"Well," Grandma continued, "the constable knew what people would think if they found out about the soot marks, so he kept that quiet. He was not a superstitious man and he knew there had to be some other explanation. Maybe the dead stranger had friends in the area who were trying to get revenge for his death. This seemed more plausible than the man's charred hand running around killing people. So he got his other deputy and some of the townsmen, and they rode around looking for strangers. But they found no one.

"That night, the second deputy, mourning the death of his friend, walked aimlessly around town, reeling from the shock. He was walking home after midnight when his scream woke half the town. Lanterns flared to life as people rushed to their windows to see what was going on. They saw the deputy lying facedown in the street. Those who got to him first, including the town doctor in his nightshirt, rolled him over. His dead eyes were wide with fright, and his throat was streaked with soot.

"The next day, stories of the Crispy Hand were all over town. It crept the streets at night, they said, and would not rest until its murderers had all felt its sooty grip. The constable redoubled his efforts to find a real, human culprit, but again he failed. By that evening, he was starting to have his doubts. Superstitious or not, all this talk about the Crispy Hand had him rattled. He was the only one left of the three who had locked up the stranger, and the sun was going down. He was scared.

"So when his wife said that she was ready for bed, he told her to go up without him. Then he made himself a full pot of strong black coffee. He made himself comfortable at the table and covered his lantern. In the darkness, he drank coffee to stay awake, keeping one hand on his gun.

"After midnight, he was starting to feel drowsy despite all that coffee. But then he heard a soft thump from the fireplace, and he was instantly wide awake, with all his senses focused to razor sharpness. *It came down the chimney*, he thought. He heard it scuttle through the ashes and scrabble across the hearth. Suddenly he threw back the cover of the lantern, and there it was."

Grandma made a sweeping gesture, and Tommy and the others flinched. Grandma had to grab at her teacup to keep it from toppling.

"The Crispy Hand was poised there on its fingers like some hideous five-legged spider. As soon as the constable rose from his chair, it skittered into the darkness behind the coal stove. Warily he approached, with the lantern dangling from one hand, and his revolver in the other. The hand scuttled away from the light, circling the stove. The constable gently holstered his revolver and picked up the tongs from the stove. The tongs clacked as he tested them, like giant iron tweezers. Then he set the lantern on the floor and began to circle the stove.

"The Crispy Hand retreated from him as before but seemed wary of the light from the lantern. As it seemed to hesitate, trapped between the constable and the lantern, the constable lunged. The tips of the tongs closed on the Crispy Hand. He lifted it from the floor and moved it closer to the lantern. Both fascinated and repulsed, he studied it in the light, a human hand, charred and blackened by fire, its skin flaked and mostly gone. But the most grotesque thing was the way it moved. Its fingers thrashed as if madly playing some invisible piano.

"Suddenly the constable could bear looking at the thing no longer. He threw open the door of the coal stove and thrust the hand in among the glowing red embers. Most horrible of all, *it would not burn*! Its fingers seemed to calm as they stirred the embers, and then it just sat there in that infernal heat as if waiting.

"The constable, growing angry with frustration, pulled out the hand and smashed it against the floor. He held it there with the tongs and stomped on it with his boots, but it did no good. The Crispy Hand seemed to be indestructible. He glared at the hand and cursed it. 'You'll not kill me, evil thing,' he vowed. And then he came up with a plan. If he could not destroy the hand, he could at least contain it so that it would not be able to creep up on him in a moment of vulnerability and strangle him, as it had his two deputies. So he put the hand into a stout wooden chest and slammed the lid closed before it could scramble out. Then he locked the chest and hid it away where no one would find it.

"And that," Grandma said, glorying in the conclusion of her tale, "is how the Crispy Hand came to be locked in the attic of this very house!"

That night Rich and Tommy slept in twin beds in the guest room. At home they had their own rooms and liked it that way, but sleeping in the same room was fun once in a while. Tommy had his penlight, and they made shadows on the wall for a while. Then they spent a long time talking and laughing in the darkness. However, they stopped suddenly when they heard a skittering sound overhead.

"Ooh," Tommy said, "do you think it's the Crispy Hand?"

Rich snorted. "No, I think it's leaves blowing across the roof."

"Do you think it really happened? That someone died in the fire like Grandma says?"

"Maybe. She must have gotten the idea for the story somewhere. But you know what? I think I've figured out why she tells us that stupid story every time we come here."

"Why?" Tommy shone his penlight in Rich's face.

"Get that thing out of my eyes, or I'm not gonna tell you."

Tommy turned off the light. "So, why?"

"To keep us out of the attic. Think about it. As scared as we used to get about the Crispy Hand, we never would have dared going up there."

"Yeah," Tommy said, seeing his brother's point. "But why wouldn't she want us to go up there?"

"That's just it. That's the real question. What's up there she doesn't want us to see? As far as I know, nobody's been up there for years. Grandma certainly couldn't make it up there. If she went to all the trouble of making up that stupid story, whatever's up there has to be pretty good."

"I guess we could go up and look," Tommy said, throwing back his covers. "The trapdoor is in the closet in this room. And I've got my penlight."

He flashed it in Rich's eyes again.

"Turn that stupid thing off or I'm going to shove it down your throat."

Tommy turned it off, snickering.

"We can't go up now," Rich said. "Mom and Grandma would hear, and we don't want them to know we were in the attic, right?"

"Right," Tommy agreed.

"So we'll wait until tomorrow," Rich went on. "Mom and Grandma are planning to go to garage sales all morning. We can say that we want to stay here and build a fort in the woods or something. While they're gone, we can spend as much time looking around the attic as we like."

"That's a pretty good plan," Tommy said. "Sometimes, you can be pretty *bright*."

He flashed the light in his brother's face again.

"That's it—you're dead!"

The boys' not wanting to go to garage sales came as no surprise to their mother, but she was still reluctant to leave them behind.

"What are you going to do here by yourselves?" she asked.

"Watch TV, eat, mess around in the woods," Rich said. "The same stuff we do at home."

"I don't want you two horsing around in your grandmother's house and breaking things."

"Naw, we won't," Tommy said. "We'll only break things outside."

Their mother sighed and looked at Grandma. "See what I have to put up with? Be glad you didn't have boys."

Grandma snorted. "No two boys could have been as big a handful as you and your sisters. It's okay if they stay here. They won't get into any mischief, right boys?"

The boys were reassuring as they hustled the two women out of the house. They watched through the window until the car was out of sight.

"Let's go!" Tommy shouted, racing for the closet that held the trapdoor to the attic. He got to the hallway before he realized his older brother wasn't following. "What are you waiting for?"

"I was just thinking about the way Grandma looked at us. She trusted us not to cause any trouble."

"We're not going to cause any trouble," Tommy said. "We're just going to go up into the attic and look around." Then a grin spread across his face. "Unless you're scared. Think the Crispy Hand is going to get you?"

They stared at each other for a moment. Then they both ran for the guest room. Rich caught up to Tommy on the stairs and practically ran over him to get there first. They opened the closet packed with old coats and clothes wrapped in plastic. Above the hanger rod was a wooden shelf holding a few dusty boxes. In the ceiling was the trapdoor.

Rich and Tommy got a chair. With help from his brother, Tommy climbed from the chair and got one foot on the shelf in the closet. Then he pulled himself up until he could push through the trapdoor and poke his head into the attic. It was a lot warmer up here and smelled like an old sweater. A little light came through a vent at one end, but it was mostly dark.

"Get out of the way," Rich said as he lunged through the trapdoor. For a moment they were both wedged there until Tommy wriggled free. Then he got out his penlight and shined it around. The bare rafters came together overhead and sloped down toward the front and rear walls of the house, like an upside-down V. The floor was made of planks laid across the rafters below, although they were hard to see through the clutter of boxes and junk.

"So what is it we're not supposed to see?" Tommy asked.

"I'm not sure yet," Rich said. "Shine that light over here—*not* in my face."

There were bundles of old magazines and newspapers, an antique sewing machine, boxes of glass jars, coffee cans full of rusty nails, mottled paint cans, a plug-in plastic Santa Claus, ancient suitcases, and a manual typewriter. The boys looked through it all but found nothing promising until they came across an old military footlocker that had their great-grandfather's name and "U.S. Army" stenciled on it.

"Cool!" Tommy said. "What do you think is in it?"

"How should I know?"

Rich went to open it but found it locked with a hasp and an old rusted padlock. He grabbed the lock and twisted. It came off in his hand.

"Whoa, look out Superman!" Tommy shouted.

"It was so old, it just fell apart," Rich said, shaking the rust off his hand. Then he pulled the hasp open and lifted the lid. Both brothers leaned forward to peer in. The beam of the penlight showed them . . . nothing.

"It's empty," Tommy said with disappointment.

Rich grabbed the penlight and probed every corner, but the only thing he found was a hole in one side a few inches across. "Looks like rats took whatever was inside."

Tommy heard a soft thump from the closet beneath the trapdoor and froze. He could tell from the look on Rich's face that he'd heard it too.

"Mom and Grandma?" Tommy whispered.

"They shouldn't be back this soon," Rich replied in similarly hushed tones. "But if they catch us up here . . ."

Rich and Tommy scrambled back through the trapdoor, got it closed, shut the closet door, and put the chair back. Then they investigated the mysterious thump. However, the house was now completely quiet, and the car was still gone from the driveway. They decided something must have fallen over and went outside to play in the woods.

The boys' mother and grandmother didn't get back until late that afternoon, with a car full of bargains. After unpacking and examining their purchases, they took the boys out to dinner and then to the movies. It was late by the time they got home, and after the long day they had all had, they soon went to bed.

Tommy was exhausted and didn't have the energy to zap his big brother with his penlight more than once or twice before falling asleep. But not long after dozing off he was awakened by a scuffling sound on the rug near his bed. A lifetime of hearing about the Crispy Hand electrified him with fear. He scrambled for his penlight and flashed it wildly across the floor.

And there it was! Just as Grandma had always described, the Crispy Hand was poised there on its fingertips like some hideous black spider. Its charred skin glistened under the light, and it retreated a little.

Then Tommy noticed something else taking shape behind it. He was reluctant to move the flashlight beam off the hand, but it turned out that he didn't need to. The figure materializing in the center of the room glowed with a light of its own, a pale and eerie illumination like moonlight. It was a man, tall and hairy and clothed in a bulky coat that hung poorly on his thin frame. Tommy recognized him from the story—it was the stranger who had died in the jail. With still-mounting terror, Tommy realized that the right sleeve of the coat hung empty.

The stranger looked right at Tommy . . . *and smiled.*

Too frightened to move, Tommy watched as the stranger crouched down to the Crispy Hand. His empty sleeve brushed against it, and a ghostly hand emerged and joined with the man's arm. The Crispy Hand crumbled in a small pile of ash. The stranger stood, flexing his newly rejoined hand, and—after once more smiling at Tommy—faded away to nothing.

It was a minute before Tommy could even move. He just lay there, frozen in fear, his penlight shining on the spot where the Crispy Hand had been. Finally, he snapped out of it. "Rich! Wake up! Did you see that?"

Getting no response, he shined the penlight in his brother's face. But this time he received no threats or warnings. Rich did not move to shield his face. His bulging eyes did not so much as blink as they stared lifelessly at the ceiling. His slack mouth hung open. And his neck was streaked with sooty finger marks.

Suddenly Tommy knew why the ghostly stranger had been smiling. The Crispy Hand had been unable to kill the constable all those years ago and complete the stranger's revenge. But tonight it was finally able to fulfill its mission of vengeance—by killing the constable's great-grandson instead.

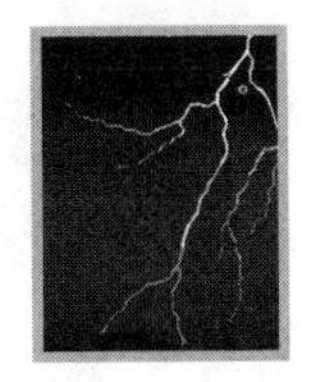

DREAM CATCHER

Anne Bancroft Fowler

Raven Scollcroft opened his backpack and dumped the contents onto his sleeping bag. The dream catcher took a bounce and floated away, like a Frisbee borne on a breath of summer air.

Raven grabbed for it, hoping no one else had seen, but he was too late. Twelve pairs of curious eyes watched it go up, then start to drift lazily down.

"What is that thing?" Raven's new friend, Marc, asked in a puzzled voice.

The Scout troop was out for the weekend, camping overnight on the shores of Lake Superior. When Raven's grandmother had heard about the trip, she'd insisted on giving him her own personal dream catcher to take along. "You must use it there," she warned. "Powerful spirits walk those woods."

"Hey, Raven!" Kurt snatched the dream catcher out of the air and held it out of reach. Its feathers ruffled in the morning breeze. "What'cha got there?"

"Just give it back, Kurt." Raven clutched at it in vain.

"In a minute! Let me take a look!" Kurt held the webbed circle to his eye and peered through an inch-wide hole in the middle. "What is this, some kind of Indian charm?" Kurt shifted the feathered treasure to a position above his head and he hopped from one foot to the other, in an imitation of Indians he had seen in the movies. Some of the Scouts laughed.

It made Raven want to deck them all, but it was too late. His secret was out. He could look forward to another summer of kids like Kurt putting him down with their ignorant stereotypes.

Raven had been teased about his name as long as he could remember. And when people learned of his Native American ancestry, it always got worse. He was only part Indian, and during the winter he lived in the city with his white father, where he conveniently ignored his heritage. But summers he spent with his Grandmother Noko, one of the few remaining full-blooded Ojibwa Indians. She lived on the reservation and followed the old ways, as did most of her friends.

"Back off, Kurt," Marc said, coming to Raven's support.

Raven grabbed Kurt's arm and tore the dream catcher from his hand. They stood glaring at each other.

"Break it up, boys. We're here to learn about the outdoors." Mr. Johnson, the Scout leader, came out of the woods and dumped an armload of firewood on the ground. "Kurt, see if you can get this fire going, and Raven, I need you and Marc to help me set up the archery target."

"Okay," Raven mumbled. A smirking Kurt moved away from him. Raven examined the dream catcher carefully. No feathers were missing, as far as he could tell. Grandmother Noko would never forgive him if he brought it back damaged. It had been careless of him to dump his pack out with a bully like Kurt standing by.

He smoothed the catcher and put it back in his pack before he ran to where Mare and Mr. Johnson stood waiting in the clearing. Together they set up the archery target, then Mr. Johnson sent Raven and Marc back to the campsite for bows and arrows.

"Well?" Marc asked as soon as they were out of earshot.

"Well, what?" Raven said defiantly.

"How come you didn't tell me about that thing? I thought we were friends." He paused and pointed to Raven's backpack. "What is that *thing* you have in there, anyway?"

Raven sighed. "That thing belongs to my Grandmother Noko. She's very superstitious."

Marc looked puzzled. "What's it supposed to do?"

"Noko thinks the night is filled with dreams, so she keeps her dream catcher hanging by the bed to catch them as they float by. The good dreams get through the hole in the center, and the bad dreams get tangled up in the feathers and disappear the next morning."

"She really believes that?"

Raven shrugged. "She believes a lot of strange things. It's hard to explain."

"What about you?" Marc asked, with a slight smile on his face.

Raven shook his head. "Are you kidding? Of course not!"

Some of Noko's ideas did make sense to Raven. At least, he could understand why she believed in them . . . but a dream catcher? He didn't think so.

The rest of the morning went by peacefully, filled with woodcrafts and nature study. The troop hiked to the top of a waterfall in the afternoon, and that night they roasted hot dogs and marshmallows over the open campfire.

After clean-up, Mr. Johnson took Raven aside. "I heard Kurt teasing you earlier," he said, eyeing him thoughtfully. "Don't ever be ashamed of who you are, Raven." Then he returned to his seat by the fire and gathered the troop around him.

"Lake Superior plays a big part in the history of this area," Mr. Johnson told the other boys. "Did you know that the shores of Gitche Gumee in the first line of Longfellow's poem *The Song of Hiawatha*, refers to Lake Superior?"

Mr. Johnson droned on, but Raven didn't hear a word he said. He knew Indian lore inside out and backwards from listening to his grandmother. His head spun with stories of Gitche Manitou, the Great Spirit, and Manabozho, the son of the West Wind. That was all Grandmother Noko ever talked about, and he pretended to be interested. But the truth was, they were nonsense to him, no better than fairy tales.

Finally Mr. Johnson finished his tale on Native American history and announced it was time for lights out.

Raven was glad. He zipped into his sleeping bag next to Marc and immediately started to drift off to sleep.

"You awake?" Marc asked.

Raven yawned. "Barely."

"Well, I was wondering what you did with your grandmother's dream catcher."

Raven opened one eye. "I put it away. Why? You want to use it?" The boys laughed together. "I don't like being made fun of," Raven said, by way of explanation. "So nobody's going to see that thing again . . . at least not on this trip." he added, unaware of how he would soon come to regret his decision.

No sooner had Raven fallen asleep than he began to dream. It was night, but the moon lit his path as he ran through the forest where the Scout troop had hiked earlier that day. He was alone, his feet skimming silently over the ground without disturbing a leaf. Coming to the edge of a clearing, he paused to stare at a small herd of grazing deer.

Automatically, he dropped his bow from his shoulder and reached behind his head to draw an arrow from his quiver. Then he stopped and looked down at himself in surprise, suddenly aware that he was dressed in traditional Indian garb, with a bow and arrow in his hand.

I'm dreaming, he told himself within the dream. *And*

it's a happy dream, the kind of good dream Grandmother Noko caught in her dream catcher. With a little laugh, he quickly placed the arrow in the bow and took careful aim. Then it happened.

A shadow fell across the grass, like a dark cloud passing before the moon. Startled, the herd of deer looked up, pranced a few steps in alarm, then darted off in every direction.

Raven lowered his bow in disappointment. He gazed up at the heavens, trying to determine the size of the cloud. *Would the deer return when it had passed?* he wondered.

The dream continued, but the content was clearly beginning to change.

Suddenly, an enormous figure lumbered onto the scene. It towered over the clearing and completely blocked out the sky. Raven recoiled in his sleep and tried to wake himself up. Standing erect on two legs like a man, the beast had the head of a wild boar, with sharp, tusklike fangs jutting from its lower jaw. Its immense, bear-shaped body was covered with fur. From its clawed hands, jagged sparks of electricity shot forth like lightning bolts.

"Raven!" the beast called to him. "I have come to teach you your fate. It does you no honor to lie hidden in the trees," it growled. "Come into the clearing where I can talk to you!"

Frightened, Raven dropped his bow and arrow and turned to run.

"Stop!" the beast commanded.

Raven ran all the faster, but not fast enough to escape the bolt of blue ice that sizzled from the monster's claw. It was a huge jolt of power that penetrated Raven's heart, knocking him to his knees. He gasped for breath and collapsed, feeling himself slipping into unconsciousness.

When Raven awoke, he was confused and painfully aware of the cold that enveloped him like a shroud. He turned his head from side to side, slowly realizing that he was at the campsite. The fire was almost out, but in the dying embers Raven could see the sleeping figures of the Scouts around him.

"Wow, what a dream," he murmured as he rooted deeper into his sleeping bag, shivering. His teeth began to chatter. *It's summer!* he thought. *Why am I so cold?*

Then he remembered the dream. Sitting up with a start, he felt strange and lightheaded. He tried to wiggle his feet and discovered that he couldn't feel his toes . . . or his fingers. *What's wrong with me?* he wondered, beginning to feel frightened.

He looked at his hands, turning them over, examining them . . . seeing right through them!

Terrified, Raven cried out in alarm, but only a rush of wind came from his mouth. *What's happening?* his mind shouted as he felt his spirit begin to drift upward toward the treetops. His spirit body, now transparent, was actually floating several feet above his solid body, which was still lying on the ground. Panicked, he called upon the one person who might know what to do. *Grandmother Noko!* he shouted in the silence of his spirit. *Help me!*

Immediately his grandmother's image appeared to him in a shower of light. "Raven!" she cried, dropping to one knee beside his solid body on the ground. "What have you done?"

Raven watched his grandmother pull back the flap of his sleeping bag to reveal his chest. Silently she pointed to the area around his heart. His chest had become as transparent as clear ice, and Raven could see that his heart was blue and covered with frost, not beating.

"Tell me what happened," his grandmother commanded.

Raven told her of his dream. She nodded wisely. "An evil spirit, a Windigo, has turned your heart to ice," she said. "I warned you to use the dream catcher. Why did you not listen?"

Raven's voice trembled with fear. "I'm sorry, Grandmother. Tell me what to do."

"There is only the old way. You must journey to the cave of the Windigo and steal some hot tallow from its candle. It will melt the ice in your heart and restore you to life. Hurry! To succeed, the act must be completed before the light of day touches your body." As she spoke, his grandmother quickly untied a length of slender rope from around her waist and thrust it toward Raven.

"Take this," she said. "It will aid you in your quest."

"Wait!" Raven cried. "Where are you going? I need your help."

"I have done all I can. I am old and must return to my body before the life force is spent," she said. "Remember, concentrate on securing the tallow to rub on your heart. Allow nothing to distract you from your task, else all will be lost."

Raven was frightened. "But what should I do? How will I find the Windigo?"

"Call on your namesake, the Raven," his grandmother said, as she began to fade. "His instinct can guide you, if you will but heed it."

As Raven watched, Grandmother Noko dissolved before his eyes, leaving only the smallest residue of light where she had appeared.

Raven didn't understand the strange command, but he was determined to obey the wise old woman. He tried to concentrate on the bird for whom he was named. *Raven*, he said in his mind. *Raven, Raven, Raven*.

Suddenly he heard a great flapping of wings. An enormous black bird, larger than a man, swooped down from the sky. It landed on the ground a few feet away. *Why have you called me?* The bird's voice rang in Raven's thoughts. Frightened, Raven didn't answer at once, and the great bird began to gather its wings beneath it for flight.

Wait! Raven shouted in his mind. *I need your help!* He

quickly told the giant bird all that his grandmother had told him, and at the bird's command, he climbed upon the raven's broad wings.

Looking down on the forest below as they rose into the sky, Raven realized that his spirit body had become one with that of the great bird. And, now, in the form of the bird itself, Raven circled once to get his bearings. Then, following his instincts as Grandmother Noko had advised, he flew directly north, toward the land of perpetual ice and snow.

Vast stands of timber and great waterfalls dotted the landscape below, as Raven soared through the sky. Then the vegetation began to change as he came upon snowcovered mountains. The trees were short and stubby, with scrubby clumps of needles growing from their stunted limbs.

Raven flew on. The air grew colder as he reached the edges of the glaciers, where huge sheets of ice covered the ground and had done so since before man walked the earth. Here Raven turned east, for he suddenly, remembered from the many legends his grandmother had told him that the Windigo lived on a glacial island all his own.

The moon had begun to sink in the sky before Raven saw the entrance to the cave. Carved in a wall of ice, the hole was almost hidden beneath an overhanging cliff. *This is the home of the Windigo you seek*. Raven could hear his grandmother's voice whisper in his mind, as clearly as if she were there. *Go there now. Save yourself.*

Separating his spirit from his carrier, Raven signaled the great bird to land on a narrow ledge directly above the hole. Once there, he lowered himself carefully down the face of the ice cliff by means of Grandmother Noko's rope and swung his legs into the hole.

As soon as he let go of the rope, he realized that there was no floor beneath his feet. He plunged through the darkness for several minutes before he hit bottom with a thud.

Immediately he sprang to his feet, then crouched, fearful of being discovered. Nothing happened. Not a breath of frigid air stirred to signal a waiting presence. The only sound he heard was a distant trickle of water, like the runoff of slowly melting ice. After a few moments, his eyes adjusted to the darkness, and Raven straightened up to look around.

He was standing in the center of a great ice chamber, a huge cavern that appeared to be several miles high and just as wide. Along the sides, he could see hundreds of crystalline blocks of ice, each square frozen around a darker core. Raven realized there was something oddly familiar to him about the shapes at the center of the blocks, but he had no time to examine them now. *Allow nothing to distract you from your task*, he heard Grandmother Noko's warning echoing in his brain. *Else all will be lost.*

At the end of the great cavern, a tiny light flickered in

the darkness. It looked like the flame of a candle, and Raven moved cautiously toward it.

Suddenly, he heard a thundering crash and felt the ice tremble beneath his feet. Terrified, Raven ran quickly to hide behind one of the ice statues. After a few seconds, a giant figure lumbered into sight, holding before it an enormous candelabra with 12 burning candles. It was the Windigo!

Crouching behind the block of ice, Raven watched, trembling, as the beast approached. It stopped a few short yards from where he hid. Holding the candelabra at an angle, the Windigo allowed a few drops of hot wax to fall from a candle onto one of the statues. Immediately, the icy outer shell melted away, and the body of a young Native American girl fell to the floor. Raven could see that her heart was encased in blue ice, just like his own in the body he had left by the campfire. But as the tallow hit the girl, her eyelids fluttered, and she began to regain consciousness.

In a flash, the Windigo tore a piece of flesh from her arm. The maiden screamed in horror and tried to pull away, but the Windigo ignored her. Holding the candelabra with one hand and dragging the terrified maiden behind it with the other, the Windigo began to tear her body apart, limb by limb, devouring the pieces as it walked back to the farthest reaches of the ice palace.

Raven remained concealed among the ice statues, shuddering. He now understood what fate awaited him if he could not get the hot tallow and make his way back to the camp before dawn.

He had lost all track of time, but he knew he must act quickly—his life depended on it. As soon as the Windigo disappeared in the distance, Raven ventured out from his hiding place and ran after the beast, who had vanished through a huge arched doorway of ice.

Reaching the archway, Raven stopped long enough to calm his racing mind, then cautiously stepped into the icy cave beyond. In the flickering candlelight, he could make out the figure of the giant resting its head on a table at the far end of the huge cavern. He started in that direction, then nearly collapsed with fright as he heard a deep rumbling.

Frozen in his tracks, Raven stared at the monster until it dawned on him that the beast had fallen asleep and was snoring! Creeping along the wall, shaking at each of the beast's thunderous snores, Raven finally approached the table. Standing on tiptoe, he reached for the heavy candelabra. It tipped in his grasp, causing a drop of hot tallow from the candle to spill onto the Windigo's furry skin.

"Aaargh!" the giant yelled in pain as it awoke. Looking around, the monster spotted Raven. It leaped up from the table with a roar, sending a bolt of blue lightning sizzling toward Raven's head.

Clutching the candelabra to his chest, Raven ran for his life. As he dodged between the ice blocks in the great cavern, bits of tallow from the candles splashed on the frozen forms. Instantly, their outer shells fell away, and figures emerged, moaning and crying for help. Roaring angrily, the giant paused in its pursuit of Raven long enough to blow its freezing breath on every stirring figure, turning each back into a frozen statue.

Panting with fear, Raven made it to the far end of the cavern—only to discover that there was no door, no exit from the cave. The hole through which he had fallen into the cavern was high above his head, too high for him to reach, and the wall was too steep and icy for him to climb. He felt a tremor like an earthquake shake the ice beneath his feet and heard the heavy footsteps of the approaching beast. *Concentrate on a way to get out of here!* Raven told himself. He focused his whole mind on seeing himself astride the raven once more.

Suddenly, Grandmother Noko's rope miraculously slid down the ice wall beside him. Raven looked up. His namesake had received his silent message, for there, holding the rope firmly in its beak, was the giant black bird. Quickly, Raven looped the rope around his waist and began to pull himself up the slippery ice, the candelabra still firmly in his grasp.

The Windigo was close behind. Raven felt its frigid breath on his neck as the beast's claws clutched at him. Turning to face his foe, Raven held the candelabra before him, thrusting it into the monster's face. The beast fell back with a horrified roar, as hot wax splattered on his skin, giving Raven just enough time to scramble up the ice wall to the waiting bird.

Outside the entrance, Raven rolled all the remaining tallow into a ball and stored it in his mouth before he once again climbed aboard to blend his spirit form with that of the great bird. Then he took flight, the tallow protected in his beak.

It was almost dawn as Raven looked down from the sky above the campfire. He saw that the Scouts were awake, gathered around Mr. Johnson, who administered CPR to Raven's still form. A stricken Marc knelt by his side.

A short distance away, the contents of Raven's back-pack lay scattered on the ground, and Kurt leaned over to pick up Grandmother Noko's dream catcher.

"No!" Raven screamed, seeing the dream catcher in Kurt's hand. His cry came out as the screech of a raucous bird. Kurt looked up in surprise.

"Don't touch that!" Raven shrieked again, diving on Kurt and flapping his great wings in an effort to drive him away from his grandmother's prize.

Kurt dropped the feathered object and backed away in alarm, but as Raven opened his beak to screech again, he could no longer hold the precious tallow in his beak, and it fell directly onto the dream catcher. It burst into a great ball of flame just as the sun broke over the horizon, its early rays touching the cold body of Raven Scollcroft.

And in that moment, the mortal Raven Scollcroft died. For without his grandmother's sacred dream catcher, there would be no return from the other world of his consciousness. He was trapped forever in the world of his dreams . . . and nightmares.

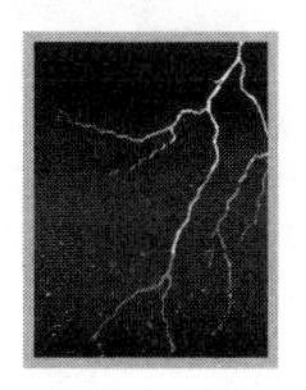

BLOODY LAUNDRY

R. C. Welch

The morning sky was dark with the promise of a coming storm. Ellen couldn't stop shivering as she waited for her friends, Cybil and Nola. The three of them always walked to school together, but this morning Ellen wished she'd gotten a ride from her mom instead. It looked like they were going to get drenched. Finally she saw the two girls approaching from farther down the street.

"Come on, you guys," she shouted as she took a few steps toward them. "I'm freezing to death!"

"Don't be such a wimp!" Cybil called back. "This is spring weather where I come from in Chicago."

"They say it's going to snow later today," Nola added in her usual serious tone as they drew closer.

"Well, I don't care if it does." Ellen fell in beside her friends. "As long as I don't have to be outside in it."

As if in response to Ellen's comment, a light rain began to fall. Huddling under their umbrellas, the three girls followed their usual path through the woods.

During the summer, this was the best part of the day. Ellen loved walking through the cool shade under the trees, following the crooked stream that flowed there. But today the bare branches looked like dead claws, and everything was eerily silent, except for the faint dripping of rainwater off the tree limbs. Although nobody said anything, all three girls felt the strange silence and walked a little faster than they normally did. Then they all stopped dead in their tracks when they saw a figure bending over the edge of the stream ahead of them.

"Who's that?" asked Cybil, pointing at the crouching figure. "I've never seen her before."

Ellen peered through the misty gloom at the old woman. It looked like she was bending over something in the water. "What is she doing out here on a horrible day like this?" Ellen wondered out loud.

"Weird," muttered Nola. "Let's go around her."

Ellen nodded her agreement. Something about the whole situation was odd, and she suddenly felt nervous.

As the three girls began to edge off the path, Ellen, who didn't want to startle the woman, called out "Hello" to her as they came closer.

She didn't answer, but Ellen was now close enough to see the woman's greasy black hair and the faded, shapeless dress she was wearing. Unbelievably it looked like the woman was doing her laundry in the stream. Ellen was about to make a comment to her friends when she saw what the woman was washing and her words caught in her throat. She was washing clothes so stained with blood that the part of the stream where she knelt was a pool of red. There was blood streaked on the woman's arms up to her elbows, and tiny fingers of red slipped into the current, washing downstream.

Ellen stopped abruptly and heard Cybil and Nola stumbling to a halt behind her. She heard one of them gasp as they also got a glimpse of the horrible sight.

"Do you think she killed somebody?" demanded Nola in a shrill voice, backing away. Although Nola had spoken loudly, the woman gave no sign that she even noticed the three girls.

"I don't know," whispered Ellen.

"Well, let's not stick around to find out," insisted Cybil. "Let's get out of here!"

The girls broke into a run. Stumbling over roots, dodging tree branches and prickly bushes, the three friends fled in the direction of their school. Every few feet, one of them would cast a panicked glance over her shoulder to see if the horrible laundress was chasing after them, but she seemed to have vanished in the mist.

Ellen broke out of the trees first, with Nola and Cybil close behind, then together they raced across the meadow to the safety of the school football field. Erin Smith, the teenage daughter of the PE teacher, was jogging around the dirt track that circled the field. Ellen called out as they ran toward the older girl.

"What is it?" Erin asked in alarm when she saw their panicked faces. "What's the matter?"

"We saw . . ." Ellen gasped, "we saw something horrible back along the stream."

"It was an old woman," added Nola in a breathy voice. "And she—"

"She was washing clothes covered with blood!" Cybil finished.

Erin's eyes widened in disbelief. "What?" she asked. "What exactly did you see?"

Ellen had recovered her breath by this point and attempted to tell their story as calmly as she could. When she finished, she shuddered with the awful memory.

"And the old woman never said a word," Nola added. "She never even looked up."

Erin considered what she'd just heard. Then she looked at the three girls with confidence. "I know what you saw," she said. "You've just described a *Bean-nighe*."

"Ben Neeyeh?" asked Cybil, puzzled by the strange word.

Erin nodded. "Yeah, I've heard about them from my grandmother. They're supposed to be the ghosts of women who died in childbirth. They're fated to wash their bloody laundry until the day when they normally would have died."

The three friends looked at one another in disbelief. "But what does it mean?" Ellen asked. "Why would we see her there all of a sudden? We walk the same way to school every day and have never seen her before."

Erin glanced over their heads toward the forest. Then she leaned forward and whispered slowly, "The *Bean-nighe* is only seen by those who are about to die."

"What?!" Ellen yelped, backing up a step.

Cybil put her hands on her hips. "Yeah, right!" she scoffed.

Erin straightened. "You're the ones who brought her up, not me."

"But," Nola protested, "we all saw her. What does that mean?"

"I don't know," answered Erin with a shrug. "Maybe it only counts for the one who saw her first."

In spite of her skepticism about Erin's story, Ellen felt an icy layer forming around her heart. "But—but who was that?" she stammered.

"Oh, come on!" Cybil exclaimed angrily. "This is crazy. It was probably some old beggar woman." She looked up at the sky, now almost black. "We're about to get soaked, and first period is starting. I'm outta here." And with that she stormed off toward the school.

Deciding that she was probably right, Nola and Ellen said good-bye to Erin and followed their friend to class.

"Erin's just trying to scare us," Nola whispered.

"Yeah," Ellen whispered back, hoping that Nola was right.

The rain grew stronger throughout the day, and lightning filled the sky. By the end of the afternoon, icy hail was coming down in sheets. Rather than walk home in the downpour, Ellen called her mom at work to see if she could drive her and Nola home. Cybil, who truly loved the cold weather, decided she'd rather walk.

"Watch out for the bloody laundry lady," Ellen joked. During the day, they had come to agree with Cybil that all they had seen was a beggar woman washing her clothes. Now they were convinced that what they thought was blood was only some kind of wine or food stain.

"In this weather?" Cybil asked with raised eyebrows. "No laundry is *that* important!" She burst out laughing and headed for the forest.

By the time Ellen sat down to dinner, the hail had turned to snow. "Looks like we're in for a real blizzard," her dad said as he came to the table after watching the news.

"Really?" Ellen asked, a faint stir of excitement running through her at the thought of school being canceled. "I sure hope—"

But the ring of the telephone interrupted her, and she excused herself to answer it. It was Cybil's mother, asking if she'd seen Cybil. "She never came home from school," the worried woman said. "Please, Ellen, can you tell me where she is?"

But all Ellen could offer was the news that Cybil had decided to walk home after school by herself.

Over the next few hours, as the wind rose and the snow began to fall more heavily, policemen searched the neighborhood for Cybil. Her body was found within a few hours, lying halfway in the stream in the woods.

"They say she probably slipped and fell," Ellen said in a tense telephone conversation with Nola after the initial shock had worn off. "She must have hit her head on a rock or something, and froze to death before she came to."

"Do you really believe that?" Nola asked.

"What do you mean?" Ellen returned almost defensively. "Of course I do. Don't you?"

"It just seems so . . . sudden," Nola answered. "I—I don't know what to believe."

They were both silent for a moment, thinking of their friend. Then Nola asked hesitantly, "What about the woman we saw this morning?"

"What about her?" Ellen demanded harshly. She wasn't about to admit that the same thought had already crept into her head. She had been relieved that if Erin *had* been telling the truth, then at least they now knew who had seen the washing woman first. Sure it had made Ellen feel disgusted with herself for thinking such a horrible thing, but she *had* to admit she was glad *she* wasn't the one who was found dead in the stream.

"Well," Nola continued, "maybe the woman we saw really was that *Bean-nighe* thing Erin was talking about."

"And you're happy Cybil was the one to see it first?" Ellen said, accusing her friend of her own selfish thought.

Nola sounded shocked. "No! I'm wondering if Erin was right. Maybe the curse counts for *everyone* who sees the woman!"

Now Ellen felt really scared. "Look, Nola, Cybil's mom said the police told her it was an accident. That's good enough for me." She searched for an excuse to hang up. "Anyway, I've got to get off the phone now. My mom wants to use it."

"Okay," Nola said, unconvinced. "I'll see you tomorrow . . . I hope."

By morning, thick drifts of snow had piled up overnight, and the radio announcer reported that her school would be closed for the day. Ellen's wish had come true, but her parents weren't so lucky. Their offices were both staying open, so Ellen asked her dad to drop her off at Nola's house on his way to work.

By unspoken agreement, neither of the girls mentioned the strange woman they had seen the previous day. Still, they couldn't help talking about Cybil and how much they missed her.

By mid-morning, the snow began falling again, and soon after, while Ellen and Nola were watching TV, the electricity went out. With a groan, Nola picked up the phone to call her parents, who had also gone to work.

That was when the girls realized the phone lines were dead, too.

"Now what are we going to do?" Ellen wondered out loud, a feeling of panic slowly rising within her.

"How about making some lunch, then going out back and building a snow fort?" suggested Nola, who didn't seem to be bothered at all.

"Yeah!" exclaimed Ellen, immediately forgetting her fears. "Maybe we can get some of the other kids from the block to come over so we can have a snowball war!"

Soon they were happily hunched over peanut butter and jelly sandwiches, cracking each other up with silly stories about some of last winter's snowball fights. Ellen was in the middle of describing how she pounded one of the boys from their band class when Nola began making a strange sound.

"What?" Ellen asked, thinking the other girl was trying to say something. 'I didn't understand you."

Gagging uncontrollably, Nola pushed herself away from the table. That's when Ellen realized something was terribly wrong. Her friend's face was turning a bright red, and her hands were clutching helplessly at her throat.

"Nola!" Ellen screamed. She tried pounding on her friend's back, but Nola's horrible choking only became worse. In desperation, Ellen grabbed her friend from behind, wrapped her arms around Nola's chest like she had seen on TV, and squeezed.

But nothing happened, and Nola's face was now changing from red to blue and her lips were turning a horrible shade of purple. With her veins swelling on her forehead as if they were about to pop, Nola fell to her knees. She turned an agonized face toward Ellen, then fell to the floor in a deadly silence. Then her body relaxed, and the color completely drained from her face.

"Nola?" Ellen said in a small voice. Then she screamed, "No!" and ran out of the house.

She had no clear idea of where she was going. All she knew was that she had to get away from her friend's body, and all she heard over and over again were Erin's words: "The *Bean-nighe* is only seen by those who are about to die."

Suddenly feeling the cold air going right through her thin turtleneck, Ellen realized that she had run out of Nola's house without her jacket. Panicking, she looked around. It was hard to recognize where she was. Everything was white, and the swirling snow made it impossible for her to see more than a few feet in front of her. To make matters worse, with the electricity down there were no streetlamps or house lights to form landmarks.

"I am *not* going to die!" she said out loud to no one. "It's just a coincidence. That's all it is—a horrible coincidence."

She began walking in what she thought was the right direction toward her house, but before long she was shivering so hard her teeth were chattering. She tried to angle herself toward the sidewalk and ended up stumbling into a street sign. By squinting, she could barely make out the letters, and she happily realized that she was about five blocks away from home. *No problem*, she told herself. *I've done this walk hundreds of times before . . . but not in weather like this.* Ignoring her traitorous thoughts, Ellen struggled forward toward what she hoped was her house.

Soon her world narrowed to the patch of snow directly in front of her feet. She walked like an old woman, bent over and shaking, breaking into fits of coughing, and murmuring the word *coincidence* over and over again.

When she finally reached her own street, it felt as if a huge weight had been lifted from her. She broke into a quick shuffle as she hurried toward the warmth and safety of her home. Before she knew it, her yard was in front of her, and she ran up the front walk and flung herself through the door. It took a long time for her numbed brain to register that the house was dark. Then she remembered that the electricity was dead.

First things first, she thought as another spasm of coughing clenched her chest. She stumbled down the dark hallway to the bathroom and reached into the medicine cabinet for the cough medicine. She knew from experience that the taste was horrible, so she quickly gulped down a couple of mouthfuls.

Suddenly pain shot through her with such intensity that it pitched her to the floor. Her throat began to burn, and her stomach felt like it was being torn apart. She tried to scream, but the walls of her throat had swollen shut. Her weakened body flopped on the floor like a fish out of water, and her vision dimmed. Whatever she had swallowed, it wasn't cough medicine.

Then, like a hideous joke, the lights flickered back on—just in time for Ellen to see that she had drunk from a bottle of her mother's hair dye. *Coincidence—yeah, right!* was her final, mocking thought before the poisonous liquid took her.

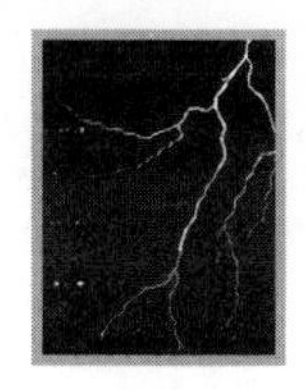

THE LAYOUT

David Dorion

Mikado, Mikado, Mikado," Winston said. "What?" I asked.

Winston pulled some kind of paperback from his back pocket. "This is my code book," he said. "And what I was saying was a new chant I just learned." He pointed to the neighbor's tabby, then said the words again: "Mikado, Mikado, Mikado."

"So what are you trying to do with this chant?" I asked.

He gave me a goofy grin. "The cat will show up later," he said.

"What do you mean, it'll 'show up later'?" I wanted to know. We were in his front yard, and the cat in question was next door, stalking birds. It was Saturday, and my mom got this bright idea for me to come over and hang out with Winston, "that nice new boy," as she called him. All the other kids on the block called him "the spaced-out kid," among other names, like nut-boy and Weirdo Winston. I told my mom I didn't want to hang out with him, but what I meant to say was, I'd rather disappear altogether than be seen anywhere with Winston Coswell.

Anyway, obviously I ended up going over to his house, and after sitting around listening to him name the genotypes of all the worms crawling through his lawn, and after being bored to death by his endless talking about what he found last week in the condemned apartment building on Third Street, he started with this weird "Mikado, Mikado, Mikado" chant.

I shrugged, not knowing and not really caring what he was saying, but I was sort of intrigued by that code book of his. It was black with a gold locomotive on the cover, and inside the engineer's cab was something that looked like a ghost or skeleton working the controls. Still, in the end, though Winston's code book did hold my interest for a moment, I found I really didn't care about it either.

I looked across the street, spotting Old Man Rancid's dachshund beside the mailbox on the corner. He and his dog were alike: mean and snarling. Hating both of them, I picked up a dirt clod from Winston's mother's oleander garden, pulled my arm back, and aimed.

"No," Winston said, reaching for my wrist.

"No?" I asked, raising my eyebrow.

He got up, also looking at the dachshund. "Let's do the chant instead."

I looked at Winston like he was nuts. I had a clear shot at the old man's miserable little dog—a bull's-eye. No chant could do the damage a good dirt clod could do. But Winston was already halfway across the street, so I let the dirt clod fall to the ground and followed him. He stood in front of the snarling dog, who now bared its pointy little teeth.

"Mikado, Mikado, Mikado," Winston said, pointing to the hot-dog-shaped animal.

Suddenly Old Man Rancid's front door squeaked open. He hobbled across his porch on his bad leg that everybody said was made out of wood and shook his fist at us. "What are you doing to my dog?" he shouted, his milky eyes wide and glaring at us.

Winston stood his ground and said the chant again.

I looked at the dog, who just panted, growled, and looked back and forth from Winston to me as if deciding which one of us he should bite first.

Winston said the chant a third time.

"You brats!" Rancid's voice rattled like a chainsaw. "I'll have both your hides if you don't leave my dog alone!"

"Let's go," I told Winston, starting back across the street. "*Now!*"

I didn't run, I just walked fast back to his house. I didn't want Winston to think I was afraid of the old man or his dog. But in a way, I was.

"Cool, huh?" he asked when we reached his lawn.

I looked at Winston like he'd lost his mind. "What do you mean cool?" I demanded, sorry I didn't nail the dog like I planned. I picked up another dirt clod, but instead of hurling it at the dog, I threw it high in the air and watched it fall down and explode in the street. Then I looked at Weirdo Winston. "Let's do something," I said, bored out of my mind. "And stop with that stupid chanting business, okay?"

"Maybe they're not there yet," Winston replied.

I groaned. "What are you talking about?" I asked. "You don't know if *who* are *where* yet?"

"The cat for one," Winston answered. "I don't know if it's on the layout yet."

I could have punched Winston, I was so frustrated. But before I had a chance to even think about lifting my fist, he looked at his watch, then suggested we go to the basement to see his train layout.

"Oh, I get it," I said, figuring out that the layout Winston had been blabbering about was what his train tracks were on. I still had no idea what he meant by the cat being on it, but I decided there was only one way to find out. "Okay, Winston, my man," I said, trying to sound cool. "Let's go check out this train layout of yours."

It wasn't like Winston and I were close or anything—after all, the guy teetered on the edge of nerd oblivion—but I have to admit the train layout he showed me was amazing. In my eyes, it actually saved him from his geekiness.

With mountains rising clear to the ceiling, and covering the entire length and width of the basement, Winston's train layout was huge. At the foot of one incredibly real-looking mountain was a church, houses, and other buildings. And on just the other side of an awesome-looking tunnel was a field that looked like it actually had real stalks of corn growing in it. In fact, the whole basement looked like a small town with train tracks running through it in some kind of bizarre maze. I followed the track, almost getting dizzy as it wrapped around mountains, climbed over green hills, and disappeared into tunnels.

Winston calmly walked over to a chair, adjusted his thick glasses, and flipped a switch on the transformer.

Instantly the landscape came to life. Lights glowed in houses, cars moved down the street. But what was more fascinating were the little plastic people. I mean, they were stepping off curbs, walking past store fronts, and hopping over fences.

"Watch this," Winston said, his eyes gleaming. He flipped another switch on the transformer. Slowly a locomotive and passenger cars began moving from a station.

"So—so where's the cat?" I stammered, finally finding my voice. "You said something about it maybe turning up on the lanscape." I blinked my eyes, making sure the incredible scene before my eyes wasn't just my imagination. "The cat . . ." I mumbled. "Where is it?"

Winston peered through his thick lenses, then finally pointed over a boulevard to the roof of a house. "There," he said. "Look."

I couldn't believe it. There was a cat that looked just like the neighbor's tabby in miniature form. But then my rational mind kicked in. Sure it was a cat. But Winston could have picked it up from any hobby store and put it where it was. Except for one thing—the cat jumped off the roof.

"Cool, Winston," I said, feeling the air leak out of my lungs. I couldn't decide whether to run or just accept that I'd lost my mind.

"And look!" Winston pointed to a street corner. "There's Old Man Rancid's dog."

I stared in disbelief at an exact replica of the snarling dachshund we'd seen only minutes earlier.

"How?" I gasped. "How did you—"

But just then, Winston's mother's voice floated down from the floor above. She was saying something about what she intended to make for dinner.

"No broccoli, understand?" he called back, almost as if he were making a threat. Then he looked at me. "Pretty cool, huh?"

Needless to say, I decided that Winston was very cool indeed. I ended up spending hours with him, totally mesmerized by how he'd say that weird Mikado chant, and without fail animals and various objects would suddenly appear on his train layout. Then, as if things weren't already pretty strange, they got even stranger.

It all started when Al DeMarco and Mickey Picasso, these two bullies at school, decided to make me their next target. They'd never really liked me much, but I knew they meant business when they cornered me against the fence by the football field.

"Heard you've made friends with the new nerd," Al said, latching onto my shirt and pulling me closer to him.

"Yeah," said Mickey. "I guess that means *you're* a nerd, too." He grinned. "Well, here's how we treat nerds."

And with that, Al and Mickey went after me. I guess I was lucky to walk away with only a fattened lip. I guess I was lucky to walk away at all. But there was one thing I didn't have to guess at—Winston was off limits to me if I wanted to stay alive.

So at lunch, I didn't eat with him like I had for the last week. And I ignored him completely for the next couple of days, not even turning around when he called out to me. But no matter what I did, Winston didn't get the point. He tagged behind me until finally I turned on him at the tether ball court and got right into his face.

"Why are you following me?" I snarled.

"I know what they did," he said matter-of-factly. "I heard Al bragging about it to some of the other guys."

I felt humiliated. Clearly rumors were already spreading about what a wimp I was. I looked away from Winston and studied my shoes.

"I'm sorry they hurt you, but I won't let that happen again," Winston said. "We're friends."

"You can't do anything about them." I swallowed hard as I fought back tears. "They're twice your size."

"I can use my chant on them," he said flatly. Then he turned on his heels and walked away.

I remembered the weird feeling I'd gotten when I'd seen the cat and the dachshund on his layout. Then I thought of the even weirder feeling I got when Winston had sort of threatened his mother, and my blood ran cold.

"Hey, Winston!" I yelled. "Wait!"

But he just waved me away. "Come over after school," he said, not looking back. "They'll be there."

Winston's parents were home when I showed up at his house after school. They looked tired, as if neither had gotten any sleep.

"He's downstairs," his mother said, waving toward the basement. "What's going on down there, anyway?"

"Don't bother them," Winston's father said. "They have important business."

I glanced at Winston's father and shivered at the fear in his eyes. Then, without saying another word, I headed down the steps to find Winston. What was happening with his parents wasn't my problem. Al and Mickey, and whatever Winston had done to them—*that* was my problem.

When I entered the basement, Winston was wearing a blue-striped conductor's cap, and he had already gotten the trains running.

"What's wrong with your folks?" I asked, not wanting to find out about Al and Mickey just then.

"They don't know what to fix me for dinner," Winston answered, with no trace of emotion in his voice. He watched a freight train clatter across a bridge, then gazed upward at another train as it wheezed around the tight corner of a mountainside. "Come here a second."

I stepped up to the layout, and for a moment I just stared at Winston as he watched his trains. There was a strange smile on his face. A look as if he had done something tremendous, yet secretive.

"I can't stay," I said. "My mother's on me about my homework."

"I've done mine," Winston said absentmindedly.

"So where are they?" I finally blurted. "You said to come over after school and they'd be on the layout."

"Look there," Winston said. He kept his eyes on the train as it negotiated the mountain, and pointed toward a school at the same time. "Look by that fence near the football field."

I peered down. Glued onto the black asphalt was a fence that ran around a football field that looked exactly like the one at our school. Next to the fence were two boys, their arms spread, their hands curled into fists.

"Wow," I muttered. "It looks just like them."

"I know," Winston said, smiling his weird, nerdlike smile. "Pretty cool, huh?"

I looked down at the tiny replicas of two boys, then leaned in closer for a better look. One boy had blond hair—Al's blond hair. The other wore a red and white shirt—the *same* shirt Mickey always wore.

"It's them, isn't it?" I asked, suddenly feeling a little sick to my stomach.

Winston adjusted his glasses and pulled on his red conductor's cap. "You could say so."

I looked back at the tiny figures of Al and Mickey. They were against the fence, frozen. They looked scared to death.

"They're not moving or anything," I said.

Winston nodded. "I know they aren't."

The trains continued circling, moving in and around the town, in and around the mountains. But I kept my eyes on what was supposed to be Al and Mickey.

"Let's watch with the lights off," Winston suggested.

I really didn't want to. In fact, I didn't think Winston's layout was cool anymore. Instead, it was starting to get creepy—no, now it was downright scary.

"I'll only keep the lights off for a minute," he coaxed.

"Okay," I agreed, not wanting to upset Winston since he was getting sort of scary, too. "But only for a minute."

He reached for the wall switch, pulled it down, then sat down and flipped another switch next to the control panel. Instantly small lights that looked like tiny stars showed up on the ceiling, while below, street lamps, lights in buildings, and car headlights all came on. I was in awe. I could even see people sitting inside the passenger train chugging by.

"Isn't this great?" Winston asked, his finger pushing up his glasses. "It's like a little world. It's *my* little world."

"You're right," I said, squinting at houses with cars pulling into driveways, and people standing on street corners ready to step into crosswalks.

"I know I am." He looked back at the trains, at their headlights playing ghostly shadows. "This is what they're seeing," he said, gesturing to the tiny people on the layout. "This is what Al and Mickey are seeing—a train passing, cars slowing at an intersection, and stars above them."

"I—I need to get home," I stammered.

"Okay," Winston said, shrugging. "If you have to. Of course, I don't *have* to do anything." He paused, then grinned at me. "Hey, bring a list to school tomorrow."

"A list?" I asked. "Of what?"

"The people you hate," Winston replied, emotionless.

I left as fast as I could, blowing past Winston's mom, not even answering her question: "What does Winston want for dinner?" I didn't know what he wanted, and I didn't care. All I wanted to do was get home.

As I raced toward my house, I saw Old Man Rancid still scouring the street and calling his dachshund's name. I passed him like a tornado, sure that he thought I had something to do with his missing pet. And now, in a way,

I guess I had to agree with him. I knew who made his little dog disappear and where it was. I just had no clue how Winston had managed to pull off the whole thing. The only thing I was sure of was that it had something to do with that bizarre chant and that even more bizarre code book.

I crossed the Connally's lawn, streaked over the Thompsons' driveway, and dashed through my back door. I found my parents waiting, but instead of fuming about my leaving the house without finishing my homework, both Mom and Dad rushed forward, their arms open.

"Oh, honey, thank goodness you're here," cried my mother. She was all over me with hugs and kisses.

"What's going on?" I said, trying to fight her off.

"Al DeMarco and Mickey Picasso," Dad said.

"What about them?" I asked, sure that I already knew the terrible truth.

Mom sniffled. "They're missing."

The next day the whole school was buzzing about Al and Mickey's disappearance. Though I felt sick inside, I had to admit I didn't mind not seeing them in the cafeteria plotting their next bout of bullying. The truth is, I was delighted they weren't around anymore, so delighted that after gym class I met Winston and gave him my list.

"This'll be way cool," I said, looking around the schoolyard, knowing that some of the kids there might as well have had bull's-eyes painted on their backs. "Really cool," I said.

Winston folded my enemy list and put it into his front pocket, then took the code book out of his back pocket and patted it fondly. "Hey," he said. "What are friends for?"

That night at dinner, all I could do was push the food around my plate, hardly taking a bite. My parents didn't notice, though. They'd brought the portable TV into the dining room so they could catch any news about Al DeMarco and Mickey Picasso.

Feeling both excited and very alone, I went to my room. The list I'd given Winston was long. I'd written down the names of people I'd hated since kindergarten, and after that, I'd listed the names of their pets. Lying on my bed, I stared at the ceiling. Through the window I could hear Old Man Rancid's growling voice from the street, still calling for his dog.

When I finally heard my parents go into their bedroom, I quietly crept down the stairs and out the back door. Then I ran like crazy to Winston's. It wasn't until I was around the corner from his house that I felt two hands reach out and grab me by my shoulders.

"Where's my dog?" a gruff voice growled at me.

I turned around and looked into the angry eyes of Old Man Rancid, but I was speechless.

"Where is he?" he demanded.

"I don't know," I lied.

The old man let go of me, but he also stepped forward. "You do know, you little brat. You do. But what you don't know is that my dog was all I had in the world. That dog *was* my world." He shook a meaty finger at me. "And I know what you boys are up to. I know exactly, and I wouldn't want you to make me do something we all might regret."

"I didn't touch your dog!" I yelled.

"But you know something about him," the old man insisted. "Don't you?"

I stepped back. "I don't know a thing." Then I faked left, then right, and dashed straight for Winston's front porch. After frantically ringing the doorbell and pounding on the door, I couldn't believe it when nobody answered. Then I tried the knob, only to find that it was unlocked.

As I crept through the dark house, feeling my way toward the basement, my heart thundered in my chest. I don't know if I was scared out of my wits or just plain excited, but I couldn't wait to see Winston . . . and the layout.

"It's done," he said, turning around to see me standing in the basement doorway.

"Old Man Rancid, he—" I gasped, not able to talk yet. "He just grabbed me and—"

"I just finished," Winston interrupted. "Don't worry. I got everybody on your list."

I looked at the layout. There were people all over it—sitting, standing, lying down, and leaning. And there were animals, too—dogs, cats, birds, even hamsters—all scurrying about or sitting in people's laps being petted. The layout was crowded, very crowded, and everyone I wanted to be there was there.

"Ready?" Winston asked.

I was about to ask, "Ready for what?" but I didn't get a word out before he stood up and hit the light switch, plunging the room into complete darkness. Then he sat back down and threw the switch that set all the little lights blinking.

"It wasn't easy," Winston said, smiling at me. "You had a long list. But I finally finished."

"Well, I'm *not* finished," a voice boomed.

The voice wasn't Winston's, and it wasn't mine. It was deeper, *much* deeper than either of ours, and much older.

"I'm not finished with you little brats," the voice snarled, and then the overhead light flashed back on.

There, up in the doorway, stood Old Man Rancid, his cracked face stiff and solid like a wall of wrinkles.

I froze. I could hear my insides buzzing, my voice

building inside my throat until finally my words burst out. "The chant, Winston!" I yelled. "Say the chant!"

But Winston didn't say anything. He just sat there, paralyzed, staring wide-eyed, not at Rancid, but at the book in the old man's hand—his code book.

"That's right," the old man said, holding the paperback book up for Winston to see. "I've got your precious code book." He gazed fondly at the black and gold cover, then looked at Winston. "I saw you drop it while you were running with your friend there across my lawn."

Winston only blinked, his mouth making small movements like he was trying to speak but suddenly couldn't.

"Did you think no one else could read this?" An evil smile came over the old man's face. "Well, it just so happens that I was a train buff when I was a kid, too. Fact is, I still am. Funny I didn't recognize that chant you were saying at my dog—not until I remembered that it was the name of a locomotive." He patted the book. "Now with this code book of yours, the whole thing has really come together for me."

I stared at Winston. Did he say "Mikado" three times or four? Did he say it five times or six? I may not have cared when I first heard it, but I sure cared now.

"You know," the old man taunted, creeping down the basement stairs one step at a time, "I have a layout, too, though it's nothing like this. Mine's just track and a train. An oval, actually." He stopped talking as he squinted at the backyard of one of the houses on Winston's layout. "Why, look at that," he said. "I think I see my dog down there."

That was when Winston suddenly found his voice and shouted—no, he screamed—the first two Mikados. But Old Man Rancid was faster, and *his* voice was louder.

"Mikado, Mikado, Mikado," his voice thundered.

In a flash, Winston was gone.

Then the horrible old man looked at me.

"No!" I pleaded.

But all Old Man Rancid did was wink.

"Mikado, Mikado, Mi—"

I found myself standing next to Winston in a desert. At least that's what it looked like—a flat, arid desert, with no mountains, no sun, no sky. In the distance, I heard the shrill whistle of a train, followed by the thunder of its moving weight. Then, far across the flat layout, I spotted the locomotive. I tried nudging Winston but couldn't move my arms. I couldn't turn my head, either. Whether or not he could, I still don't know to this day. All I know is what I see—the train passing around, fading off, then coming back again and again and again.